# BY THE GUN

Richard Matheson showcases his brilliant imagination in this unforgettable collection of tales of the outlaws and heroes who lived, fought, and died in the Old West . . .

"A MASTER STORYTELLER."

**—Joe R. Lansdale, Award-Winning Author of *Dead in the West* and *The Magic Wagon***

"COMPELLING AND HISTORICALLY ACCURATE."

***—Publishers Weekly***

"MATHESON'S VERSATILE TALENT IS ALMOST LEGENDARY . . . REGARDLESS OF GENRE."

***—Ellery Queen's Mystery Magazine***

And now, Richard Matheson once again proves his storytelling genius with a daring novel of the Old West that will ignite your imagination . . .

# SHADOW ON THE SUN

*Berkley Books by Richard Matheson*

JOURNAL OF THE GUN YEARS
THE GUNFIGHT
BY THE GUN
SHADOW ON THE SUN

Spur Award–Winner

# RICHARD MATHESON

After a long, successful career in the fields of horror, fantasy, and science fiction, legendary author Richard Matheson turned his remarkable talents to one of his favorite genres—the Western. His first Western novel was an incredible success, the winner of the Golden Spur Award for Best Western Novel of 1991 . . .

## JOURNAL OF THE GUN YEARS

An epic adventure from the diary of Marshall Clay Halser, a gunfighter who lived up to his legend . . . and died for it.

"THE BEST NOVEL I READ LAST YEAR."

**—Stephen King**

"*JOURNAL OF THE GUN YEARS* KNOCKED ME OUT. IF EVERY WESTERN WERE THIS GOOD, I'D READ NOTHING BUT WESTERNS!"

**—Dean Koontz**

"BREATHTAKING . . . FIRST-RATE . . . IMPOSSIBLE TO PUT DOWN."

**—Spur Award–Winner Richard Wheeler**

"A THREE-CARAT DIAMOND. READ AND ENJOY IT WITHOUT DELAY."

**—Max Evans, Winner of the Levis Strauss Golden Saddleman Award**

"A SPECTACULAR CREATION."

**—Dale Walker, Columnist, *Rocky Mountain News***

"THE AUTHOR GIVES HIS STORY A CREDIBILITY AND HONESTY UNUSUAL IN THE GENRE."

**—*Publishers Weekly***

"SOME OF THE BEST DAMN WRITING MATHESON'S DONE IN A SPECTACULAR CAREER."

**—Loren Estleman, Author of *Bloody Season***

***Turn the page for more rave reviews . . .***

# THE GUNFIGHT

Richard Matheson's powerful novel of a young girl's idle gossip—and the explosive reaction of a small town—that leads to dishonor and death . . .

"TIMELESS HUMAN DRAMA . . . IMMEDIATE AND COMPELLING."

—***Booklist***

"PAGE-TURNING . . . THIS IS AN ABSORBING PARABLE about the terrible effects of gossip and the tragedy of a peaceable man driven to violence."

—***Publishers Weekly***

"ANOTHER WESTERN TRIUMPH FOR RICHARD MATHESON."

—**Spur Award–Winner Norman Zollinger**

"RAW, ROUGH, AND REAL."

—**Loren Estleman**

"SUPERBLY WRITTEN SUSPENSE!"

—***Library Journal***

"SURPRISING AND MOVING . . . AN EMINENTLY SATISFYING PIECE OF WORK."

—**Spur Award–Winner Chad Oliver**

"REAL PEOPLE, PLOT TWISTS, AND AUTHENTIC WESTERN COLOR . . . A VERY, VERY GOOD BOOK."

—**Ed Gorman**

"A DECEPTIVELY SIMPLE PREMISE . . . AN UNFORGETTABLE CHARACTER . . . MATHESON MAKES EVERYTHING WORK."

—**Dale Walker, *Rocky Mountain News***

# SHADOW ON THE SUN

RICHARD MATHESON

BERKLEY BOOKS, NEW YORK

SHADOW ON THE SUN

A Berkley Book / published by arrangement with
RXR, Inc.

PRINTING HISTORY
Berkley edition / November 1994



ISBN: 0-425-14461-5

BERKLEY®
Berkley Books are published by The Berkley Publishing Group,
200 Madison Avenue, New York, New York 10016.
BERKLEY and the "B" design
are trademarks belonging to Berkley Publishing Corporation.

PRINTED IN THE UNITED STATES OF AMERICA

10 9 8 7 6 5 4 3 2 1

I dedicate this book to my dear friend Chad Oliver.
See you later, pal.

# SHADOW ON THE SUN

# WEDNESDAY

# One

A MILE OUTSIDE of Picture City, they had set up a tent for the meeting with the Apaches. A troop of cavalry from Fort Apache had been dispatched to the conference, and now two lines of horsemen faced each other on the cloud-darkened meadow—one line the saber-bearing cavalrymen; the other the blanketed Apache braves, impassive-faced, sitting their ponies like waiting statues.

Everything looked drab and colorless in the gloomy half-light—the grass and bushes drained of their late autumnal richness, the horses dark or dun, the costumes of the soldiers and Apaches composed of solid, cheerless hues. Only here and there did color show—lightly in the weave of a blanket, more boldly in the slashes of yellow stripe along the dark pant legs of the cavalrymen.

Between the lines stood the tent, its canvas fluttering in the cold, October wind. Inside its small interior, six men sat on folding stools: Braided Feather, chief of the Pinal Spring band, 287 men, women, and children; his son, Lean Bear; Captain Arthur Leicester, United States Cavalry; Billjohn Finley, United States Indian agent for the area; David Boutelle, newly arrived from Washington, D.C., as observing representative for the Department of the Interior; and Corporal John Herzenbach, who was there to write down the conditions of the treaty between the government of the United States and Braided Feather's people.

Finley was speaking.

"Braided Feather says that his people must be allowed to sow and gather their own grain and work their own sheep and cattle herds," he translated to the captain.

"This is their prerogative," said Leicester. "No one intends to deprive them of it."

Finley interpreted this for the Apache chief, who was silent a moment, then replied. Finley translated.

"He says it is known to him that many Apaches in the San Carlos Reservation have had their fields destroyed and their livestock taken from them," he said.

The captain blew out breath, impatiently.

"His people are not going to the San Carlos Reservation," he said.

Finley spoke to the Apache chief and, after a pause, Braided Feather replied.

"He wants to know," said Finley, "how his people can be sure they will not be sent to the San Carlos Reservation, as so many—"

"They are being given the word of the government of the United States of America," Leicester broke in pettishly.

Finley told Braided Feather and was answered. He pressed away the makings of a grim, humorless smile and turned to the captain.

"The Apaches," Finley interpreted, "have heard this word before."

The two young men sat among the high rocks, one of them looking out across the meadow with a telescope. From where they were, the tent was only a spot on the land below, the facing horsemen only two uneven lines that almost blended with the grass. Only with the telescope could the one man make out features and detail.

If Jim Corcoran had raised the telescope a jot, he would

have seen the buildings of Picture City, dull and faded underneath the cloud-heavy sky. As with the horsemen at the conference, two lines of buildings faced each other across the width of the main and only street.

If Jim had turned and climbed the steep incline behind them to its top, he might have seen the dot of Fort Apache sixteen miles due west and, perhaps, caught sight of the smoke from White River chimneys eighteen miles northwest. He would have seen, too, surrounding him like a dark green island in a sea of desert, vast forest land, and, in the distance, the snow-crowned peaks of Arizona's Blue Mountains.

But Jim was only interested in the conference taking place below. Earlier, he'd talked his older brother Tom into leaving the shop to come out and watch it.

"By God," he said, lowering the telescope, "I never thought we'd see the day ol' Braided Feather'd get to feelin' peaceable."

"We never would've either," said Tom, "if it hadn't been for Finley."

"That's right enough," said Jim. He raised the telescope again and chuckled. "Christ A'mighty," he said, "an honest Injun agent. They're as hard to find these days as honest Injuns."

His brother grunted and glanced up briefly at the leaden sky. Each time he looked at it, it seemed to have descended lower.

"She's gonna start to pourin' soon," he said. "We'd better hightail us back to town."

"Aw, let's wait awhile," said Jim. "The meetin' can't last much longer."

"Jim, they been a hour already," said his brother, checking his watch. A raindrop spatted across the gold case, and he wiped it off on his coat sleeve.

"See, there's a drop already," he said. "We'll get soaked."

"Just a mite longer," said Jim, looking intently through the telescope. "We can ride back fast if she starts up."

Tom put his watch away and looked over at his brother. When was Jim going to grow up? he wondered. He was eighteen already, but he still acted like a kid most times. It made their older brother Al mad. Well, that was nothing much, Tom thought, smiling to himself. What *didn't* make Al mad?

Tom yawned and drew up the collar of his coat.

"Suit yourself," he said. He'd wait a little longer anyway. "Can you see good?" he asked.

"Yeah, real good," said Jim.

Overhead, there was a swishing sound.

"All right, all right," Captain Leicester said irritably. "Any breach of treaty on our part releases his people from the agreement. Good God, what does the man want?"

He aimed a stony gaze at the clerk, then looked back suddenly, interrupting Finley as the Indian agent began translating for Braided Feather.

"That goes both ways, of course," he snapped.

When Finley turned again to the Apache chief and his son, he saw that, although they had not understood the content of Leicester's words, his tone of voice had been apparent enough. There was a tightening twitch at the corners of Lean Bear's mouth, the faintest additional glitter in the dark eyes of Braided Feather.

Finley pretended not to notice. He nodded to the two Apaches, then asked a question. The chief sat in silence awhile; across the table from him, Leicester shifted restlessly, the wooden stool creaking beneath his weight.

Then Braided Feather nodded once, curtly, and his son

grunted, lips pressed together. Finley turned to the captain.

"It is agreed then," he asked. "The band will be supervised by an Apache police force?"

"We have already discussed that," said Leicester.

"Further," said the agent, "that the band will be subject only to Apache courts and juries to be formed?"

"Presuming that the members of said courts and juries are acceptable to the United States government," said Leicester.

"They will be formed with that stipulation," answered Finley. "The point is: The Apaches must be allowed to govern themselves and, when necessary, act as their own judges, mete out their own punishment."

"Presuming that this right is not used merely as an excuse for laxity of discipline," said Leicester, "it is acceptable."

"They will govern themselves then," Finley said.

Leicester nodded wearily.

"Yes, yes," he said. He turned to the clerk. "Put it down," he said.

Corporal Herzenbach dipped his pen point into the vial of ink. The sound of it, as he wrote, was a delicate scratching in the tent, just heard above the flapping of the canvas.

Over the distant mountains, thunder came rumbling at them like the chest-deep growl of some approaching beast.

"Come on, let's get out of here," Tom Corcoran said. "It's gettin' set to bust wide open."

"Aw, just another minute," pleaded his brother, the telescope still pressed to his eye. "You talk as if we was a hundred miles from town."

"The way it's fixin' to rain," said Tom, "we could get ourselves soaked in two seconds."

"Y'think maybe the meetin's takin' so long because it

ain't workin' out right?" asked Jim, changing the subject so they wouldn't go right away. He wasn't in the mood for riding back to town just yet. Al would just put him to polishing rifle stocks again.

"Y'think so?" he asked again.

"Who knows?" Tom said distractedly. "Who the hell can figure out an Injun's brain? Braided Feather's been turnin' down treaties more'n ten years now. Wouldn't surprise me none he turned down another."

Jim whistled softly. "That wouldn't be so good," he said. "Braided Feather's a real son of a bitch. I'd hate t'see him on the warpath again."

"Yeah," said Tom. "Come on, let's go."

"Y'think maybe—what're ya lookin' at?"

Tom Corcoran was squinting upward. "I thought I heard somethin'," he said.

"Heard what?"

"I don't know."

"Where, up there?" Jim looked up at the cloud-roiling sky.

"Yeah."

Jim snickered. "I expect it was a bird, Tom," he said.

"Yeah, sure, you're funny as hell." Tom lowered his eyes and shivered once. "Come on, let's beat it."

"Oh . . ." Jim Corcoran stuck out his lower lip. Well, no help for it, he guessed. It was going to be a working afternoon and that was the size of it.

"So," he said, shrugging, "let's go then."

The sound passed overhead again, a faint, rushing sibilance.

"There it is again," said Tom, looking up.

"I didn't hear nothin'," said Jim.

"You wouldn't." Tom lowered his gaze.

Jim chuckled, standing up.

"You scared o' birds?" he asked.

Tom flat-handed him on the arm, and Jim lost his balance, almost dropping the telescope. He laughed aloud as he staggered.

"*Birds*," he said.

Below, their horses nickered restlessly. They strained at their ties.

"It is agreed then," Finley told Braided Feather in the Apache tongue. "No rifles or pistols will be kept by any of your people.

"When one of your men needs to hunt, he will go to the soldiers who rule the reservation. There, he will be given a weapon and a pass which will allow him to hunt for a certain time with the weapon. When the time is ended, the rifle or pistol will be returned to the soldiers.

"I have tried," he added to the chief, "to get permission for these guns to be held by the Apache police, but it cannot, immediately, be done. Later, when the soldiers understand, as I understand, that your word is good, I am sure we can get the weapons put under the control of the Apache police. Is that agreeable?"

Braided Feather nodded.

"It is agreeable," he said.

"Is it also agreeable," asked Finley, "that the making of *tulapai* will be limited so that none of your people can drink so much that they might commit an act which would break the treaty?"

Before the chief could answer, Lean Bear spoke angrily to him. Finley did not interfere in the brief exchange between Braided Feather and his son. He glanced over at Leicester and saw the captain gritting his teeth. He looked at Boutelle, who sat, legs crossed, looking at the two Apaches with hard, critical eyes.

Soon Lean Bear had relapsed into a thin-lipped silence, and Finley's gaze sought that of the chief.

"It is agreed," said Braided Feather, "if it is also agreed that no white man will be allowed to offer whiskey for sale to any of my people."

Finley passed this along to the captain, who nodded, a sour expression on his face. Leicester's stomach was upset. There was a dull pain in the small of his back, his wife had been frostily rejecting the night before, and he was sick and tired of haggling with these damned, arrogant savages.

Quickly, sensing the decline of cooperativeness in the air, Finley went over the remaining conditions of the treaty while the captain squirmed uncomfortably on the squeaking stool. The two Apaches, father and son, sat without expression. David Boutelle sat, lips pursed, appraising Finley's words, and the corporal clerk sat with the pen poised between his ink-spotted fingers, waiting for instructions.

Outside, the chill October wind rustled the browning grasses, ruffled the blankets of the Apaches and the dark coats of the cavalrymen, stirred the horses' manes, picked at the canvas of the tent, and was a cold current on which flying things could ride.

They were almost to their horses, which they had tied up in a space below the rocky shelf on which they'd sat.

"You think Al will be mad because we came here?" asked Jim. Now that they were actually going back to town, the thought of Al's angry impatience was distressing him.

"What's the difference?" asked Tom. "If he don't get mad at that, he'll just get mad at something else."

Jim chuckled nervously. "That's a fact," he said. "I think we got us the touchiest brother in the whole territory."

"Don't I know it," said Tom.

Only the week before, he'd had a fistfight with Al out

behind the shop. His ribs still ached from the drubbing he'd taken.

"Hey, I hear it now," Jim said abruptly, looking up. His gaze moved along the rock face beetling above them, but he saw nothing.

"What is it?" he asked.

"I dunno." Tom looked up, curious again. "If it's a bird, it's a hell of a big one."

"Maybe it ain't a bird," said Jim. "Maybe it's somethin' in the rocks. Y'know? Maybe a—"

It came at them with such speed that they had no chance to move. One second they were scuffling down the slope toward their horses, the next, they were paralyzed in their steps, faces frozen into masks of dumb horror. Jim was quick enough to fling an arm up, but neither of them had the time to scream.

Even if they had, their voices would not have been audible above the terrible, piercing screech that filled the air around them.

# Two

THE STORM HAD broken now. Sheets of angling rain swept across the land. In seconds, dust had become mud, dark and viscous, trees and bushes ran water from every wind-lashed leaf and twig, and the distant mountains faded from view behind a curtain of deluge. Men could not keep their eyes open in such a rain. When it struck their cheeks and brows, it stung like whip ends.

Hastily, the tent was struck and the troop rode off at a gallop for Fort Apache. It would take them at least two hours to reach their destination. By then, their uniforms would cling to them with chilling weight and the insides of their boots would slosh with water.

Captain Leicester, teeth gritted against the driving rain, led the way across the meadow toward White Canyon. Already, in his mind, he could see the day in its hapless entirety: the long ride back to the fort, his reporting the results of the conference to Colonel Bishop. The walk to his house, the slinging of his soggy-brimmed hat to the floor, the peeling off of his drenched clothes, the muttered cluckings of his wife. Then the first sneeze, the first trickle at his nostrils, the first chest cough, and off he'd be on the way to a prime cold with all its attendant miseries.

"Damn!" He let the curse go knifing into the wind-scaled rain and, for the effort, got his teeth wet. Damn it! He set his lips into a thin, trembling line. And why, he thought, *why*? For a pack of lice-infested, mule-eating Apaches!

Damn them! The sullen, staring, brooding, leather-faced savages!

Captain Leicester dug his spurs in. "Come on!" he raged. "Come on, damn you!"

When David Boutelle, wet and uncomfortable, tried to guide his horse toward the White River Hotel, a swarm of animated townsmen swept him instead toward the Sidewinder Saloon. There, along with a laughing Finley, he was virtually lifted from his saddle by the cheering men and borne aloft toward the smoke-blue, shouting din of the barroom.

As the two of them were carried through the batwing doors, a cheer went up from the assemblage. Steins and glasses were banged on tables and bar, two-fingered whistles needled at the air.

Then Boutelle and Finley were lowered jarringly to the floor and guided by their shoulders to the counter where glasses waited and Appleface Kelly, dripping rain, slammed his hamlike palm on the dark counter and bellowed for whiskey. The barroom sounded deafeningly with boot-scuffling, ragged-cheering men as they pushed happily to the counter.

When every glass and stein was filled, Appleface slammed his palm on the counter again, and, at the pistol shot report of it and Appleface's shout to "Hold it! Hold it!" everyone fell silent. Boutelle tried to get away, but he was held in a trap of smiling, eager men.

"Boys!" said Appleface. "This here's a gala day! Our wives and kids can finally walk the streets of Picture City without bein' scared of every shadow! We can work our jobs without expectin' arrows in our backs from some damn, murderin' Apache! And for that we got t'thank one man here."

Appleface beamed and pointed at the Indian agent.

"*Billjohn Finley*!" he declared.

"Hooray for Billjohn!" shouted someone.

"Right!" said Appleface. "Hip, hip—"

"Hooray!" howled the men.

"Hip, hip—"

"Hoo-*ray*!"

"Hip, hip—"

"Hoo-RAYYY!" Boutelle winced at the ear-piercing noise.

Then there was only the sound of mass, convulsive swallowing, followed in seconds by the sounds of fiery coughs, stamping boots, and thick glasses being set down heavily on the counter.

Eddie Harkness and his uncle skimmed along behind the bar, uptilted bottles in their hands, gurgling amber bourbon into the glasses. Boutelle put down his glass, still three-quarters full, grimacing at the hot bite of the whiskey in his throat. He looked around for a way out. He'd made his gesture, now he wanted to go.

"And here's to Mr. David Boutelle from Washington, D.C.!" yelled Appleface. "Hip, hip—"

"Hoo-*RAY*!"

Boutelle smiled thinly and tried to leave, but glasses were being raised en masse again and he was pressed in by the shoulder-to-shoulder drinkers. He took another sip of his drink and clenched his teeth.

Finley noticed the younger man standing in his wet clothes, and when the cheers had abated and the men had gone back to their separate groups of drinking and gaming, he worked his way over to Boutelle.

"You'd better go get yourself a change of clothes," he said.

Boutelle smiled politely. "I intend to," he said. He looked

at Finley's rain-darkened coat. "What about you?"

"Oh, I'm used to it," Finley said pleasantly. "I've slept out many a night in wetter clothes than these."

"You don't talk like a native of these parts," said Boutelle, finally getting enough room to take off his hat and shake the raindrops to the floor.

"I'm not," said Finley. "I'm from New Jersey, but I've lived here over seven years."

"Rutgers graduate?" asked Boutelle.

Finley nodded. "That's how I got this job," he said. Rutgers University was the sponsor for the Apache nation.

"I see." Boutelle slid a clean square of handkerchief from his inside coat pocket and patted at the perspiration that scored his upper lip. The hot room was beginning to reek of steaming wool. This, added to the pungent odor of cigar and cigarette smoke, made Boutelle's stomach edgy.

"Well, I've got to go now," he said, picking up his hat.

"How long will you be staying in town?" asked Finley.

"Not long," replied the younger man. "Just until the Apaches are established on the reservation."

"Uh-huh." Finley nodded. "Well, that should be about a day or two."

"Mmm." Boutelle put his handkerchief away. "We'll see."

Finley knew what the younger man was thinking, but he said nothing. Boutelle, like the majority of newly arrived people from the East, believed, quite firmly and—to them—logically, that the Indian nation was composed of treacherous savages, rarely to be taken at their word, never to be trusted. Indians were, like any wild animals, to be penned in, watched over, and kept from doing evil. Finley imagined that Boutelle was one of the legion who conceived of Indian reservations as some kind of open-air zoo.

He would say nothing, however. It was not his place to

lecture. Besides, Boutelle would be gone in two days at the latest; there was no point in risking friction. Even if he did say something, it would not likely alter Boutelle's trend of thought. Words rarely changed a young man's attitude.

"Perhaps I'll see you later in my office," he said to Boutelle.

"Perhaps, Mr. Finley."

Boutelle made his turn from the bar without noticing the approach of the small Indian. The first he saw of him was as an obstacle in his path, and he twitched back as the Indian ducked aside.

"What do you want, Little Owl?" Finley asked in the Indian tongue.

The old Apache glanced timidly at Boutelle, then looked at Finley once again, his dark eyes abject. At his right side, his hand rubbed slowly on the leg of his grease-stained buckskins as though cleaning itself.

Finley grunted once and reached into his pocket. His hand moved quickly to Little Owl's and met it, palm to palm. The gesture took only a moment, and then the small Indian was padding down the length of the bar away from them.

"Did you give him drinking money?" Boutelle asked in surprise.

"Just a loan," said Finley.

"I thought giving liquor to the Indians was against your principles."

"As a rule, it is," Finley said apologetically, "but—well, I guess I just can't think of Little Owl as an Indian. He isn't really anymore. He's a hang-around-the-town Indian, hasn't even got a tribe to call his own. He lives outside of town with his wife and children."

"At the town's expense, I presume," Boutelle said acidly.

"No, no," said Finley, lying a little. "Little Owl works during spring and fall roundups. He's a pretty good little puncher."

Boutelle glanced down the counter and saw the old, stolid-faced Apache carrying a stein of beer into the back room.

"*He* works with cattle?" Boutelle asked.

"Yes, quite a few Indians do," said Finley, taking a cigar from his pocket. He bit off the end and spit it into the gaboon. "Not that they're very good at it," he went on, smiling. "They're too timid with the stock."

He chuckled at the expression on Boutelle's face.

"You've never thought of Indians as being timid, have you?" he said, blowing out a cloud of smoke. "They are, though. They hate to take a risk, any kind of risk at all. That's why they plan their battles so carefully. That's why a chief like Vittorio has lasted so long. He figures things out to the last detail."

"You sound as though you admire him," said Boutelle. He was terribly uncomfortable in these sodden clothes and in the hot airlessness of the saloon, but it was his duty to learn as much as he could about the sort of man who was, after all, representing the United States of America.

"You have to admire a good general," Finley was answering easily, "even if he is your enemy. Didn't we admire General Lee?"

"General Lee did not foment his war."

"Neither did Vittorio, Mr. Boutelle," the Indian agent said quietly.

The younger man cleared his throat.

"I fear we differ on several essential points," he said.

Finley shrugged and grinned cheerfully. "That's what makes life interesting," he said.

Boutelle nodded curtly. "Yes. Well, I really must be

getting back to the hotel. These clothes . . ."

"Yes, yes, by all means," said Finley in honest concern. "Get yourself into a hot tub. Down some whiskey. Drive the wet right out of you."

Boutelle managed a politic smile. He knew that Finley was elated at having brought these savages to bay after more than seven years of trying. He had a right to, of course. Even if he did conceive of them as noble primitives instead of the murderous brutes they were.

"You wish to see my report before I send it off to the Capitol?" he asked.

"No, no, I'm sure it'll be fine," Finley said amiably.

"Very well." Boutelle nodded once and turned away.

Finley watched the younger man pick his way across the crowded saloon floor. Twenty-five years old, he thought, maybe twenty-six. Graduate of Yale most likely, maybe Harvard. Father in the law profession or in some legislature or both. Maybe even in Congress. Mother a society grande dame in New York City, Boston, some such place. His future a well-secured plan: politics, a proper wife and children, respectability, the quiet dignity which true wealth makes easier. The descent, more than likely, into stodgy complacence, into . . .

And, then again, maybe not, thought Finley with a self-deprecating shrug. It was unjust of him to write the young man off so easily. Was he, at thirty-seven, already taking on the dogmatism of old age? No sense in planning the poor boy's future all at once. There were always shadows in a man's personality that hid surprises. Besides, he was too happy today to feel critical of anyone. Appleface Kelly was right. It was, by God, a gala day!

Finley grinned at Kelly as the bulky man sidled up to him.

"Say that Boutelle is a stiff-neck, ain't he?" said Kelly.

"Oh, he's all right," said Finley. "What's your pleasure, you great hulk?"

Kelly ordered whiskey and put it away with immaculate speed. Flushed from drink, his face was almost to the color of his name.

Al Corcoran came in at four.

Just before he did, Finley had slipped back to his hotel room for a change of clothes. Now he was back at the saloon, chatting with Kelly.

"Somethin' I always wondered," said Appleface. "Who in Sam Hill named you Billjohn?"

"Simple," Finley answered. "My father wanted to call me Bill and my mother wanted to call me John."

"So they struck them a bargain!" said Appleface.

"Right!"

The two of them were laughing when the double doors were pushed open and the tall, heavyset man came in, dark slicker dripping. Stopping at the foot of the counter, he looked around the crowded room, his eyes coldly venomous beneath the shadowing brim of his Stetson.

When his gaze reached Finley, he came walking over.

"Hello, Al," Finley greeted him. "How'd it—"

"You seen my brothers?" Corcoran interrupted.

Finley's smile faded. "No, I haven't, Al," he said.

Corcoran's lips flared back briefly from gritted teeth.

"Anything wrong?" asked Finley.

"I just told ya," Corcoran said angrily. "I don't know where they are."

Finley nodded. "Perhaps they went out to watch the meeting with Braided Feather. A lot of—"

"Then where are they now?"

"They might have decided to take cover somewhere until the rain lets up."

"They had work t'do," said Corcoran, by the statement indicating his disagreement.

"I see." Finley shook his head. "Well, I don't know what to suggest, Al. I wouldn't worry about it though."

"No, you wouldn't," Al said bluntly. "You like Injuns."

Finley looked surprised. "What?"

"You heard me."

"I heard you, but I don't believe I—"

Finley broke off and stared at Corcoran in rising amazement.

"Al, are you trying to tell me—" he began.

"If those goddamn Apaches have anything to do with this," said Corcoran, "you can kiss your treaty good-bye."

Finley set his glass down heavily.

"Have you any reason at all for saying that?" he demanded.

"I *said* it," snarled Corcoran.

Finley pressed down the tremor of anger rising up inside him. "Listen, Al," he said, trying to take Corcoran's arm.

The brutish man pulled away.

"Al, you're wrong," said Finley. "You have no reason to—"

"They're my brothers, Finley," Corcoran said tightly.

"I know who they are, Al," said Finley. "And I'm telling you that the Apaches had nothing to do with them not showing up."

"They better show up soon," said Corcoran.

Finley's breath shook a little.

"They will, Al," he said quietly.

"They better."

Finley gestured, trying to clear the air. "Look, Al, if I can help you—"

He broke off abruptly and stood there watching Corcoran move for the doorway. He kept staring at the doors even after they had stopped swinging behind Corcoran's quick exit.

"What?" He started to turn to face Kelly.

"You think the Apaches could've—"

"*No*," snapped Finley, "I don't."

But his fingers on the glass, when he picked it up, were white across the knuckles. And after he'd swallowed half the drink, he set it down and paid for it.

"I'll see you later," he said.

"Y'need some help?" asked Appleface.

"No, that's all right," said Finley. "I'm just going to help Al find his brothers. I'm sure they're somewhere in town."

"You worried, Billjohn?" asked Kelly.

"No, no, of course not," said Finley, forcing a smile, "but Al is."

He patted Appleface's shoulder. "I'll see you later," he said.

The smile began to fade as he turned away from Kelly. Before he reached the doors it was completely gone, and all the pleasure of the consummated treaty had turned into a cold, nagging distress.

# Three

LITTLE OWL SAT wondering what his brain looked like. In his youth, he'd watched two of his older brothers kill a white man. They had picked up the white man by his feet and smashed his head open against a rock. What had spilled across the dry surface of the rock had been the white man's brains, they'd told him. It had looked grayish, wet and slippery. It was still throbbing when he touched it.

But that was long ago. He could not understand why he should be thinking of it now. He had only been a small boy when it happened. Had it meant so much to him that now, when he was old, he should sit thinking of brains and wondering what his own looked like?

Abruptly, he remembered. Last week—or was it last month?—Doctor Phil had talked to him, right here in this room behind the barroom of the Sidewinder. Doctor Phil had been drunk. He drank a lot because he, too, was often tired and wanted to forget his tiredness. And he had been here, sitting across the table from Little Owl, telling him what his brain would look like if he kept on drinking.

The old Apache could not remember what Doctor Phil had said. Something about a sponge eaten away, he thought. He couldn't recall exactly. Memories were evasive now, uncertain in time and content. As if, somehow, it had rained in his head and everything was soaked together into a common, irresolute mash.

The thought amused Little Owl. Outside it was raining—he could hear it falling in the alley beyond the window—and in his head it was raining, too. The spaces between his brain matter were like alleys between the buildings of Picture City—muddy and dark. He was destroying his brain by a rain of beer and whiskey. Yes, that was what Doctor Phil had said.

Or was it?

Little Owl opened his eyes slowly and stared at the grain of the table. He looked at the limpness of his hands lying on the table with the empty, foam-flecked stein between them. What time was it? he wondered. Was it nighttime? Or was it morning? No, it couldn't be morning because, out in the other room, he could still hear the laughter and talking of the men, the clinking of glasses, the occasional scrape of a chair leg on the floor.

Little Owl straightened up with a soft groan. He had been slouched in the chair and his back hurt. Maybe he should leave the saloon and return to his wickiup, he thought. Yes, that was what he'd do. He watched his leathery hands slide off the table and felt them settle on the arms of the chair. Pushing down, he got himself into a standing position, his legs limp and watery beneath him. Everything around him was hazy at the edges, as if he were looking through the parting in a mist. Only those things he looked at directly had any clarity of line.

Little Owl walked across the room with careful deliberation. Maybe Finley was still there, he thought. Maybe Finley would give him some money to buy a stein of beer. Then he could go back to the table again and drink some more. He liked the feeling it gave him to drink, the numb, bodiless sensation. When he was deep in it, he could return to the village in the mountains and be a boy again. He could run and laugh and wrestle in the clean, high air, ride horseback again, shoot his bow and arrow, fish in the cold, rushing streams. In memory, he could fill his stomach with roasted meat and lie, at peace, in the thick, hazy warmth of his father's wicki-up.

The old Apache stood waveringly at the back of the barroom, looking for Finley. A sinking of disappointment pressed at his stomach. The Indian agent was gone. Little Owl sighed. He should go back to his wickiup. He should bring some meat to his children. Yes, that was what he'd do.

Appleface Kelly turned at the slight tug on his sleeve.

"You scroungin' again, you mangy old bastard?" he asked, then snickered. "No more," he said in Apache. "Get out of here."

Little Owl grunted and stood there, staring at Kelly with blank, obsidian eyes. Kelly turned his back on him, and after a moment, the Apache shifted his feet and headed slowly for the doors.

Before he reached them, Finley entered.

The Indian agent's slicker glistened from the rain and his hat was soaked through. Little Owl waited while Finley took them off and hung them on a wall hook.

Finley managed a smile as he turned. "Still here?" he said in Apache.

The old Indian still waited. Finley looked at him soberly a moment, then, sighing, reached into his pocket.

"Now listen," he told the Apache. "Take this money and buy food for your children. You understand?"

Little Owl stared at him a moment, then, with a grunt, he nodded once. Taking the money, he walked past Finley and pushed through the swinging doors. Finley watched him go. Poor lost soul, he was thinking. None of the dignity of his race left. Completely off the red road. Just a part-time cowboy who spent the major part of the year cadging for drinks and sitting in silent drunkenness, looking into a past in which he was a man and not just a "damn scrounging Injun."

Appleface Kelly looked over as Finley leaned against the bar beside him and ordered whiskey.

"You find 'em?" asked Kelly.

Finley shook his head. "Not yet," he said.

It was not raining as hard as before. It came down now in straight, almost soundless curtains. The air was colder though. It made Little Owl shiver as he padded along the plank walk toward the south edge of town. He should have brought his blanket with him, he thought before remembering that, months before, he'd given the blanket in exchange for half a bottle of whiskey. Or had it been years before?

At first, he didn't notice the man on horseback riding in the same direction. When he was young, he would have sensed the man's presence instantly, long before his eyes had seen him. Now, when the muffled sound of the hoofbeats reached his ears, Little Owl started and glanced over his shoulder dizzily.

It did not come at first. Little Owl saw only the outline of a man on horseback. He turned his gaze back to the front and kept on walking.

It was only after half a minute had passed that he realized the man was following him.

The old Apache squinted back across his shoulder again, trying to see more clearly. Who was the man? Did he know him? Little Owl grunted to himself, sensing the first twinge of nervousness. He walked a little faster, trying not to show it. He'd been through this sort of thing before. There were always white men who took pleasure in trying to frighten any Indian they came across.

Only when the man rode past him and reined his horse in up ahead did the small Indian stop. He was standing at the head of an alley which ran between the post office and the bank. He stood motionless, watching the man dismount and tie the horse to a hitching post.

Then the man began to walk toward Little Owl.

The old Indian shuddered. He squinted hard, trying to make the man out, but his eyes were not good anymore and all he could see was the tall, broad silhouette coming at him. Only his hearing, still acute, picked out every detail of the man's approach—the sucking of his boots in the thick mud, the creak of the planking as the man raised his weight to it, the slow, thudding fall of the man's footsteps on the walk.

Then it began.

It was not a conscious reaction in the old Apache's mind. It was something deeper, a stirring in some long dormant center of awareness. Little Owl stood woodenly, staring at the man. Unwilled, a sound of disbelief rose suddenly in his throat. He sucked in fitfully at the cold, wet air and felt his heartbeat stagger.

The man kept walking toward him. Little Owl could see his eyes now. They seemed to glitter even though there were no lights around to be reflected. Help me, Little Owl thought; help me. He tried to cry the words aloud, but his tongue was like lead in his mouth. And even as he tried, he knew that there was no one who could help him, no one who could stop the approach of this tall, silent figure.

Little Owl began edging to the side, wordless mumblings in his throat. His lungs kept laboring for breath that would not come. It seemed as though he suffocated in some cold, dark emptiness. And the man kept coming at him with unhurried strides. No, thought Little Owl, it could not be.

*It could not be.*

Suddenly, the Apache whirled and lunged into the alley, moccasins slapping at the mud. He glanced over his shoulder with terrified eyes and saw that the man still came. A sob exploded in his throat. He tried to run faster, but he couldn't. Something was dragging at his legs. His feet were stone. Gasping for breath, he ran along the alley in a daze until he reached the fence that blocked his way. There he spun around, a dry, convulsive rattling in his throat.

The man stopped, close. He was very big, broad-shouldered, a massive statue of a man. Little Owl pressed against the cold, wet fence, looking at him. He could not speak or breathe or think. All he could do was stare with frozen eyes, unable to comprehend the horror that stood before him.

The man spoke in Apache.

"You will help me," he said.

Little Owl jerked back against the fence, a dull cry pulling at his lips. The man took a step closer. Little Owl tried to scream, but only a witless bubbling came from his mouth.

"*You will help me*," said the man.

Abruptly, the eyes rolled back in Little Owl's head and, with a gagging whine, he crumpled to the ground, landing face down in the mud.

The man came over slowly and stood beside the body. He looked down at it with unmoving eyes, eyes without emotion. Then he turned and walked back out of the alley.

Finley set his glass down. "I'm off again," he said.

"Where to now?" asked Appleface.

"Well, they're not in town," said Finley, "I'm sure of that. I guess I'll have to help Al look around outside of town."

"Is that where he is?"

Finley nodded. "He rode out about an hour ago."

The Indian agent laid a coin beside his empty glass. "See you later," he said, then smiled wryly. "Seems like I already said that," he added.

"What are you knockin' your brains out for?" Appleface asked him. "The Corcoran boys ain't your worry."

"Al thinks the Apaches are involved," said Finley. "That *is* my worry."

He punched Kelly lightly on the arm. "And I don't like to worry," he said.

"Don't get wet now," Appleface told him.

Finley chuckled. "I'll see what I can do," he said.

He walked across the room and put his hat and slicker on, then pushed out through the doors and started north toward the livery stable. Finley didn't see the tall figure coming up the walk from the opposite direction.

Inside the saloon, Kelly picked his drink up and carried it across the room to where the Dailey brothers, Lon and Earl, were playing blackjack.

"Get in the next hand, boys?" he asked.

"Sure," said Lon. "Sit down."

Kelly had barely settled in his chair when the man came in.

"Hey, hey, hey," muttered Appleface.

The Dailey brothers glanced at him, then, as Kelly tipped his head toward the doorway, they looked in that direction.

Lon Dailey whistled under his breath.

The man was big. So big that the clothes he wore, though made for a large frame, clung to him tightly, the sleeve ends high on his thick wrists, the pants cuffs riding far up on his mud-spattered boots.

"Who the hell is he?" Earl Dailey murmured.

"I never seen him before," said Appleface.

By now they were not the only ones in the saloon looking with covert curiosity at the man. He did not seem to notice it, however, or, if he did, he gave it no attention. Standing immobile in the doorway, the rain-dripping hat too high on his skull, his gaze moved slowly, searchingly, around the room.

"What in hell's he lookin' for?" Lon Dailey whispered through his teeth.

"*Who* in hell's he lookin' for?" Kelly whispered back, masking the movement of his lips with a squeezing tug at his nose.

"I'm glad it ain't me," whispered Earl Dailey.

Appleface squinted at the man suddenly.

"Is he an *Injun*?" he wondered aloud.

The three of them looked carefully at the man. Strangely enough, they couldn't tell if he was an Indian or not. If swarthiness were the only test, there would have been little doubt. But they had all seen white men burned by the sun to a similar pigmentation. It was the features themselves that weren't right. The arrangement of them did not place a definite stamp of Indian on the man. Nor was he clearly a white man either. The harsh angularities of his face seemed, in fact, to go beyond the limits of either possibility. Somehow, it seemed closer to being an animal than a human face.

As the man started toward the counter, the collar of his coat slipped down.

Only the general noise in the room kept Appleface's voice from being heard as he said, "*Holy jumpin' Christ*!"

Around the entire circumference of the man's neck was a red, uneven scar, thick and crudely stitched.

The three men sat staring at the stranger as he halted before the counter. They saw Eddie come walking over, saw him glance involuntarily at the scar, then with a quick, nervous swallow, force a smile to his lips and ask the man what his pleasure was.

They couldn't hear what the man was saying; only the deep rumble of his voice was audible. They saw Eddie pour a drink hastily, but the man didn't touch it. He spoke again and Eddie answered. Even from where they sat, they could see how the young bartender seemed to shrink back from the man.

Abruptly, the stranger turned and headed for the doorway.

"Say—" Eddie called after him.

The man stopped and looked over his shoulder, his dark eyes boring into the bartender's.

"W-what about your drink?" asked Eddie, trying to look affable.

The three men couldn't see the expression on the man's face, but they noticed how a muscle twitched in Eddie's cheek.

"M-my money, I mean." Eddie seemed to be speaking more from instinct than desire. His voice was not strong, but it had grown so quiet in the saloon now that everyone could hear it.

The man didn't seem to understand.

"Money?" asked Eddie. He swallowed. "For the drink?"

He held up the glass, obviously regretting that he'd spoken at all. Then, putting down the glass, he dug a coin out of his vest pocket and held it up.

The stranger looked down at his clothes. Awkwardly, he slid his big right hand into the pants pocket and drew it out, coins clutched between the thick fingers. Stepping to the counter, he dropped them, and two of the coins rolled toward the back edge of the counter. Eddie lunged for them.

"Hey, that's too much," he said.

But the man was already halfway to the doors. Eddie called after him once again, then said no more. Blank-faced, he watched the big stranger push out through the batwing doors and disappear. One of the men at the table nearest the doorway got up and peeked across the top of the doors. After a moment, he turned back and shrugged exaggeratedly to his friends.

Appleface got up and walked over to the bar, where he talked with Eddie. In a minute, he was back.

"What'd he want?" Lon Dailey asked.

"Eddie said he asked after a small man in a black suit," he said. "A man with a little beard. A man of learning."

"He asked in English?" asked Earl.

Kelly nodded. "Yeah."

"What'd Eddie tell 'im?" asked Lon.

"Eddie said he thought the stranger must've meant Perfessor Dodge," said Appleface.

"Dodge?" Earl grimaced. "What in hell would he want the perfessor for?"

Kelly shook his head. "I dunno," he said.

"Eddie tell him where t'find the perfessor?"

"I guess he did," said Kelly.

The three men looked at each other for a moment. Then Earl Dailey cleared his throat.

"What the hell," he said, reaching for his cards. "Whose play?"

# Four

HARRY VANCE SAT mumbling behind the desk of the lobby of the White River Hotel. He was mad, good and mad. Ethel had made him come out and sit there. You never knew on a night like this, she'd said. All sorts of people might be coming in for rooms. You never knew.

Well, Harry knew. Good and well, he knew. Ethel didn't think for a damn second that there'd be any extra guests that night. She was just mad about last night and this was her little way of getting even with him. She couldn't get honest mad with him, couldn't—wouldn't—tell him what was really on her mind. Oh, no, never in a million centuries! She was a woman, wasn't she? Did a woman ever tell a man what was really on her mind? Ever in the whole history of mankind?

Hell, no! She waited till the next night and then got even with him by asking him to do something she knew full well there wasn't the least bit of need to do. Like sit here in the cold, empty lobby waiting for a guest who'd never show up. Sure, that was a woman. All tricks and deceits and never an honest-to-God explanation. Never.

Christ Almighty, you'd think they were a hundred years old apiece! The way she got so mad every time he tried anything with her. A hundred damn darn years old apiece. *Christ!*

He was glaring down the black well of his thoughts when the bell over the door tinkled and a stream of cold air rushed across the lobby floor.

Focusing his eyes, Harry Vance saw the tall man entering. Then, hastily willed, a smile of calculated hospitality creased his round face, and he leaned forward as if preparing himself to leap over the waist-high counter and embrace the man in cordial welcome.

"Evenin', sir, evenin'," he said genially. Well, by Christ, they could sure use an extra guest or two. Things were darn slow this month. Darn slow.

The tall man moved across the rug slowly, his boots leaving wet, mud-streaked imprints on the carpeting. Oh, God, he hadn't wiped his feet off! thought Harry, an agony of prescience straining behind his smile. Ethel would be furious.

Well, the hell with Ethel! he decided suddenly, eyes steeling. They could have locked the place up, but no, she had to send him out to sit in the lobby and wait for a guest. Well, here was a guest, by Christ, and he was tracking up the floor. So, the hell with her. Let her clean up the damn spots!

The man stopped before him.

"Yes, sir," Harry said, swiveling the book around and plucking the pen from its holder. "Just stayin' for the night, are ya?"

The man didn't even glance at the pen which Harry held out for him.

"Dodge," he said, his voice deep, guttural.

"Sir?" Harry Vance's smile faltered a little.

"*Dodge*," the man repeated.

"Dodge City?" Harry asked. He thought he understood. The man couldn't write and was too embarrassed to admit it. He was telling Harry he was from Dodge City. Well, that was all right so long as he had coin. Harry would—

"Pro-fessor Dodge," the man said carefully.

The smile was gone. Harry's expression was removed,

impersonal. This was no paying guest.

"He ain't here," he said.

"What—room?" asked the man. He spoke as if speaking was an ability laboriously learned, a skill not altogether mastered.

"Twenny-nine," Harry said automatically. He tightened. "But he ain't here," he said. "I *told* ya. He's on one of them field trips. He's a—"

He broke off as the man turned and headed for the staircase.

"I said he wasn't in," he called impatiently.

The man began walking up the steps, boots thudding measuredly on the worn carpeting.

"Hey!" Harry squinted after the man. "I said he wasn't in!" By Christ, he was getting mad now. He'd—

*"Harry."*

Vance almost vacated his skin as the voice snapped behind him. He grunted in pain as, lurching spasmodically against the counter edge, he hurt his stomach. He whirled, indignant.

"What're ya creepin' up behind me for?" he asked.

"Who is that man?" asked Ethel Vance, pointing toward the stairs.

Harry swallowed his indignation and added it to the indigestable mass already in his frustration-bound stomach.

"I don't know," he said. "He just come in and asked for Perfessor Dodge."

"He's not in," said Ethel.

"I know he's not in," whined Harry. "I told him so."

"Then what's he going up for?" demanded Ethel.

"He's going up because—"

Harry broke off. "I don't know why he's goin' up!" he said, exasperated. "I didn't tell 'im to. He just went."

"Then you just march up there after him, Harry Vance," she ordered. "I won't have strangers walking around in my hotel."

There it was God Almighty. *Her* hotel! As if he hadn't worked like a damn horse to make it a going proposition. Just because her old man left it to her in his will. Her hotel. Christ.

"Well?" asked Ethel.

"Well?" Harry echoed faintly. "What?"

"Are you going up there?" she challenged. "Or are you just going to stand here and let him break into our rooms."

"Oh, for—" Harry twisted irritably. "He ain't no robber."

"How do *you* know?"

By Christ—the thought drove an icy needle into his heart—how *did* he know? Suddenly, he saw that man again, standing across the desk from him; tall, swarthy, with those dark, implacable eyes. Good Christ, he might even have been an Indian! And the way he spoke, almost mechanically. Harry shuddered. And he'd yelled after the man like—

"Are you *going*?" demanded Ethel.

"Yes, yes, of course I'm going," he snapped. He stepped away from his stool and lifted the counter board. Then he hesitated.

"Well?" she asked.

Swallowing, Harry lowered the board and moved over to the drawer. Pulling it out, he reached inside and picked up the loaded derringer. Ethel looked at him with nervous speculation.

"What are you doing?" she asked, somewhat less authority in her voice now.

"Well," he said, "you can't tell. How do we know who he is?"

For a moment, he felt a stir of pleasure at the alarmed expression crossing Ethel's face. Then the cold prickle of dread was on his spine again and he found himself raising the board once more, found himself advancing toward the staircase.

"Wait," Ethel said suddenly.

Harry twitched and looked around. "No need for—" he began to say, then shut up. Well, the truth of it was he was more than glad for Ethel's company. There was something reassuring about her presence for all her furies and edicts.

The two of them started up the steps.

"You didn't get his name?" she asked.

"He didn't give it," answered Harry.

For some reason, they both spoke in whispers as if, tacitly, it had been agreed between them that the stranger in the hotel was a menace.

"You—think he has a pistol?" asked Ethel.

Harry swallowed dryly. "Probably," he said. He tried to sound casual but failed.

At the head of the staircase, they turned left and moved cautiously into the hallway. They both stopped.

"*Where is he*?" asked Ethel.

Harry stared down the empty hallway. "I don't know," he murmured.

"You think he's in the perfessor's room?" she asked.

"How could he be?" countered Harry. "The perfessor always locks his door when he goes out. He has valuable specimens in there."

Ethel swallowed.

"Then where is he?" she asked.

"Maybe he thought I said thirty-nine," suggested Harry. "Maybe he's up on the third floor."

"Go look," said Ethel.

Harry tightened angrily. Oh, sure, the thought came. Go

look. As if he was a big hero or something. As if . . .

Drawing in a shaky breath, he started up the staircase. That man was awfully big. Awfully big.

At the third-floor landing, he stopped and braced himself, one hand resting on the bannister. All right, mister, his mind rehearsed sternly, what do you want up here? You got business? He swallowed again. By Christ, he thought.

He stepped forward quickly, snapping back the hammer of the derringer so that the curved trigger came clicking down to his finger.

The hall was empty.

Harry blinked. Well, what the hell? he thought. What in the blue blazes?

"Harry!"

He started violently, his heartbeat lurching so violently it felt like a horse's kick against his chest wall. Whirling, he thudded down the steps, derringer extended.

"Come here!" called Ethel. It was not exactly a call of distress, it seemed to Harry, but then you never knew how someone like Ethel might react in a moment of danger. Maybe even sudden peril would fail to alter her habit of demanding.

But she was all right, standing at the end of the hallway by the window. Harry walked toward her quickly, testing the door to Professor's Dodge's room as he passed. It was locked.

"What is it?" he asked.

"You leave this window open?" Ethel asked, and there was something in her voice other than demand, Harry noticed.

He had said no before it struck him what the import was of his saying it. He stared out the window at the precipitous drop to the street below.

"You . . . think he *jumped*?" he asked.

Ethel pressed her lips together. "That's *impossible*," she said angrily.

They both looked out the window. Could a man jump that far? wondered Harry. Wouldn't it break his legs?

Then Ethel said, "*Harry*," in a faint voice.

"What?"

"*Look.*"

His gaze fell to where she was pointing, and he saw the imprint of boot tracks ending at the window.

Harry gaped. There was a swelling in his chest and stomach as if all his organs were expanding. No, there had to be another explanation, his mind claimed instantly. No man could jump twenty-five feet to the ground nor could he climb along a wall that was devoid of footholds or handholds.

"*Of course*," he said, speaking before his mind was set.

"What?" There was a rare sound of grateful attention in Ethel's voice.

"He's in the perfessor's room," said Harry.

"But you said the door was locked," she objected weakly.

"Sure." He plunged on, unwilling to allow the sight of those boot prints to distract him. "He locked it from the inside after he went in. He must have a skeleton key."

"But—what about the window then?"

"Don't you see?" he argued. "He tried to trick us. He opened it up to make us think that was the way he left."

"I don't—" She stared at him blankly. Then, abruptly, she pointed at the boot prints. "What about them?" she asked.

"That's a trick, too," said Harry, trying to outtalk the speed of fear. "He could walk to the window, open it, then move backwards in the same prints. That's an old Injun trick."

He snapped his fingers, making Ethel twitch.

"He *is* an Injun!" he said. "I thought so when I seen him."

"An *Indian*?"

They both looked at each other intently, and suddenly Harry knew what she was going to say and it made him cold inside.

"We'll have to look," she told him.

A shuddered breath passed Harry's lips. *We'll have to look.* The words echoed in his mind.

"You have the key?" she asked.

Harry tried to swallow.

"Well, have you?"

He murmured, "Yeah."

"Then . . ."

No more to be said. The two of them edged over to the door, and Ethel put her ear against it, face twisted with concentration.

"I don't hear anything," she whispered.

"Maybe he's not there anymore," Harry said hopefully.

"Then where is he?"

"I don't know," Harry whispered pettishly. "Are all the other doors locked?"

"Yes. They—"

They both recoiled against each other as a door down the hall suddenly opened.

David Boutelle did not see them. He walked along the hall briskly and turned right onto the staircase. They heard the sound of his descending boots.

"M-Mister Boutelle," mumbled Harry.

Ethel drew in a deep breath.

"*Open the door*," she said.

"Yes," he said, although his mind said *no*.

The hand he slid into his pocket was cold and shaking.

His fingers twitched when they touched the key. He drew it out and slipped it into the keyhole. It rattled there.

"Shh!" hissed Ethel.

Harry closed his eyes. "Will you—?" he began to request.

"Open it fast," said Ethel.

And be ready to use your gun, Harry's mind completed the instruction. He drew in a ragged breath. Through the open window at the end of the hall, he could hear the rustling fall of rain, the clopping of a horse's hooves as it passed the hotel. All right, mister, his mind began again, put your hands up. You can't go breakin' into this hotel without—

He shoved the door open and jumped in quickly, gun raised to fire.

The room was empty.

It was not until immediate fear had gone that the discomfiture of the earlier dread returned. If the man was not in here or in the hall, if he could not possibly have jumped from the window to the street—*where was he*?

Harry stood in mute perplexity while his wife stepped over to the light bracket on the wall and turned up the flame.

The room seemed truly empty. Harry closed his eyes and shivered. What in the blue blazes of merry hell, he thought, is going on?

"Well, he must have gone out the window then, that's all," he said, trying to push down the fear rising inside him.

"But—"

"Who knows why?" he anticipated her. "Maybe he heard us coming up the stairs and got scared. Who knows? But he sure ain't in here."

"Harry, the . . ." Ethel swallowed with effort. "The . . . closet," she said.

Harry could not repress the groan in his chest. Was

there to be no end to the woman's alarms? Well, he was getting tired of this, he told himself casually, as if his heart were not threatening to discharge itself from place. Striding quickly to the closet door, he flung it open.

It was empty.

"There," he said. "Now let's stop this nonsense." He was so relieved that, for a second, the room swam before his eyes.

"Well . . ." she murmured indecisively.

"Ethel, he ain't *in* here," Harry said, feeling a bolt of dread that she might start telling him to look under the bed, look behind the armchair over by the window, look behind . . .

"I . . . guess not," Ethel said.

"Come on, let's go."

Ethel turned down the flame, and they went out into the hall again.

"Shut the window," she told him as he closed the door and relocked it carefully. She started down the hall, muttering to herself, "I still can't see how anyone could jump from that high."

"Well, he did," said Harry. And, by Christ, he was going to believe it, too.

When the door had closed and dark silence filled the room again, the man lifted the window and stepped inside.

He stood for a moment beside the armchair, looking around. Behind him, down in the street, a horse was trotting by and he twitched his head around. He looked at the street, raindrops inching slowly down his cheeks.

When the horse had gone, he turned back again. He walked across the room and twisted up the oil flame, the burnished glow of it crowding darkness into the corners. Then he moved over to the bureau and drew out the top drawer.

He looked down impassively at the cuffs and collars stuffed in messily, the mound of starched handkerchiefs. He opened another drawer and stared at the shirts and ties, the undergarments, the books. Abruptly, he shoved the drawers shut. These things were of no value to him.

He stood before the bureau mirror looking at his reflection—tall, copper-skinned, dark-eyed, the hair ebony-black and long. Steadily, he looked at the reflection of his carven face.

Then his hand, which rested on the bureau top, stirred and brushed against something. The man looked down. It was a specimen of gneiss rock. He looked at the veiny structure of it, then his fingers closed around it slowly and his gaze lifted again to the mirror.

He had to find Dodge. He had to find him soon. Fury began to stir in him, and he looked at the wavering reflection of his face in the mirror, at the mounting shapelessness about his features. Only the burning eyes remained steady.

As he stared, the gneiss rock, hardened by centuries, crumbled to dust between his straining fingers.

# Five

THE PENDULUM CLOCK on the wall behind his desk was just striking for the ninth time as Finley unlocked his office door and went inside.

Standing in the darkness, he peeled off his dripping slicker and tossed it on the bench beside the door, dropping his rain-soaked hat on top of it. Slowly, he removed his damp jacket and hung it on the clothes tree.

"There," he murmured.

Walking over to the desk, he lifted off the top of the oil lamp and lit the wick, turning the flame up high. Then, replacing the top, he clumped over to the stove.

There was still a bed of glowing embers near the bottom from that morning's fire. To this he added newspaper scraps and kindling until the flames fingered up brightly. Then he dropped in heavier chunks of wood. He kicked the stove door shut, pulled a chair up in front of it, and settled down with a sigh. Groaning tiredly, he pulled off his boots and dropped them on the floor. That was better.

He was just relaxing, eyes shut, deliberating whether or not it was worth the effort to get up and make a pot of coffee, when there was a single, hard rap on the door. He grunted and opened his eyes. Pushing slowly to his feet, he walked across the cold floorboards in his stocking feet and opened the door.

"There you are," he said, "I've been looking all over for you."

"Have ya?" Al Corcoran looked exhausted, his eyes rimmed with red, his face drawn and colorless.

Finley stepped back quickly and drew the door open wide. "Come in and get warm," he said. "I'll put some coffee on."

Al came in, and Finley shut the door, pulling down the shade that covered its top half of glass.

"Now look, Al," he said, turning, "before you start—"

"They ain't back yet, Finley," said Corcoran. It was almost a warning.

"I know that, Al," said Finley.

"And they ain't holed up in some cave," said Corcoran. "And they ain't out ridin' in the rain."

"Al, there are a hundred places in this area they could be," said Finley. "You can't expect to find them on a night like this. I've been out looking for them, too, and I couldn't see a thing. So—"

"So *nothin'*," Corcoran interrupted. "You gonna do anything or not?"

"Al, I've done all there *is* to do tonight," Finley told him. "In the morning, we'll—"

"In the morning be damned!" flared Corcoran. "For all I know they're lyin' out there somewhere with—!"

He stopped abruptly, breathing hard, as someone knocked on the door. Finley gritted his teeth and stepped over to it.

"Yes?" he said.

"Boutelle," said the voice.

Oh, *great*, thought Finley. This was exactly what he needed right now. Exhaling wearily, he opened the door.

"Come in," he said.

Boutelle's eyebrows raised slightly when he saw the brooding Corcoran standing there. "Good evening," he said, nodding once. Corcoran grunted.

"If you'll excuse us for a second, Mr. Boutelle," Finley said, "I'll be with you directly."

"Of course," Boutelle said crisply. He walked over to the desk, glancing briefly at Finley's unshod feet.

"Now, listen, Al," Finley said quietly, hoping Boutelle wouldn't hear. "So help me God, Braided Feather had nothing to do with this. You'll be making a terrible mistake if you think he did. It's something else. You have to believe that. At least until—"

"Why should I believe an Injun lover?" said Corcoran through this teeth.

It was only the slightest tensing of skin across Finley's cheekbones, the least flinting of his gray-green eyes, but Corcoran went rigid as if preparing for a fight.

Finley forced away the angry tension.

"We'll forget you said that, Al," he said.

"You don't have to—"

*"Al."* Finley's fingers tightened on the heavy man's arm. "Take my word on this until morning. That's all I'm asking you to do. As soon as it's light, we'll go out and find them."

He paused a moment. "All right?"

Corcoran stared at him for a few seconds. Then, jerking his arm free, he turned on his heel and walked over to the door. It slammed loudly behind him.

Finley closed his eyes and blew out a heavy breath. Then, bracing himself for the inevitable, he turned.

"Braided Feather had nothing to do with what?" asked Boutelle.

Finley felt a heavy sinking in his stomach. Dear God, now he was in for it.

"Just a small misunderstanding," he said.

"Regarding what, Mr. Finley?"

Finley didn't answer.

"I would appreciate your telling me," Boutelle said stiffly. "Anything concerning the Apaches—"

"This does *not* concern the Apaches," said Finley.

"Apparently, the gentleman who just left thinks otherwise," said Boutelle.

"He's wrong."

"Please let me be the judge of that," said Boutelle. "What *does* he believe, Mr. Finley?"

Finley sighed. Well, what was the purpose in trying to keep it a secret from Boutelle? It would only make him more suspicious. Casually, as if relating something of little consequence, Finley told the younger man about Tom and Jim Corcoran's disappearance that afternoon. He did not emphasize Al Corcoran's idea about it.

"And they haven't been found yet," said Boutelle. It was not a question.

"Let's say they haven't shown up yet," said Finley. He forced a smile to his lips. "Now, can I be of service to you, Mr. Boutelle?"

Boutelle ignored this.

"Why are you so positive the Apaches had nothing to do with it?" he asked.

Finley clenched his teeth.

"I'm positive," was all he said.

"You talk, Mr. Finley," said Boutelle, "as if no white man has ever been robbed and murdered by an Apache before."

"No white man ever *has* been by Braided Feather's people," snapped Finley.

"I suppose—"

"That was *war*, Mr. Boutelle," Finley interrupted, anticipating what the younger man was going to say. "I, myself, killed eight men during the war with the Confederate states, but I don't think of myself as a murderer."

"I suggest, Mr. Finley," said Boutelle, "that you are, with some deliberation, blinding yourself to a condition only too prevalent. I realize fully that the idea of your hard-won treaty being already broken is not a—"

"You're *wrong*, Mr. Boutelle." Finley shuddered. How long could he hold his temper? He was close to the edge now.

"It has been well established," said Boutelle, "that any number of Indians—Apaches included—periodically desert their reservations—after first collecting their government-issued supplies, of course—and rob and murder white men!"

Boutelle drew in a quick, angry breath.

"Quite periodically, Mr. Finley," he said.

Finley looked darkly at the younger man. Already, he could see Senator Boutelle standing erect and gesturing in the halls of Congress, booming out his splendidly phrased maledictions against the Western Savage. His cheeks puffed out momentarily as he blew out jaded breath. It was useless to get furious with such pomposity.

"Let's just wait before we make up our minds, shall we?" he suggested.

Boutelle's smile was the thin, supercilious one of a man who is convinced of his own opinion.

"For your sake, Mr. Finley," he said, "I hope you're right."

Finley nodded. "Now, can I help you?" he asked.

"I had meant to consult you about my report to Washington," said Boutelle. "However, under the revised circumstances—"

The younger man stopped talking as there was a faint tapping on the door. Finley turned his head and looked in that direction. "We are really popular tonight," he muttered to himself as he padded over to the door and opened it.

A short, squat Indian woman was standing there. At the sight of her, Finley's annoyed expression softened a little.

"What is it?" he asked in Apache. "Is something wrong with your husband?"

"He has not come back tonight," she answered. "I thought you would know where he is."

Finley looked unhappily exasperated. "I sent him to you," he said. "Hours ago I sent him to you."

There was a flickering in the woman's eyes. Finley rightly identified it as fear.

"He's still in town then," he reassured her. "Look for him in the Sidewinder or at the Silver Hall."

Already, he thought he knew the answer. The old Apache had taken the money given him and gone to the Silver Hall Saloon instead of going to his wickiup as Finley had told him. It would not be the first time.

"And if I do not find him?" the Indian woman was asking.

Finley smiled. "You will find him," he said.

The Apache woman nodded. "I thank you, Finley," she said.

Finley patted her shoulder as she turned away. Closing the door, the Indian agent turned back to Boutelle.

"Was that to do with those two missing men?" the younger man asked.

"No, no." Finley shook his head. "That was Little Owl's wife. She's looking for him."

"Little Owl? Was that the Indian you gave drink money to before?"

"Yes."

Boutelle smiled scornfully. "He's probably lying somewhere in a drunken stupor," he said.

The Indian agent grunted.

"Probably," he said.

Boutelle looked contemptuous. "Indians," he said.

"No, Mr. Boutelle." Finley shook his head, and his voice had an acid edge to it. "Civilization."

Little Owl's wife shuffled through the misty rain, her dark eyes searching.

Something had happened to her husband, something evil. Of that she was certain. As certain as she was of the blood running in her veins, of the heart pulsing heavily behind her breast. Last night, as she lay awake listening to the bubbly snores of Little Owl and the children, outside, high in the cottonwoods, an owl had hooted. The sound of it had turned her flesh to ice.

This morning she had told Little Owl about it. We must leave, she had said; the hooting of an owl is a bad omen. We must go to another place.

But Little Owl had only shaken his head and refused to speak of it. He had been too long among the white men. The instincts of his fathers had died in him, and he no longer believed in signs and omens. It was at that moment, as he turned away from her in silence, that she knew something would happen. Little Owl's failure to believe would cause it.

She did not enter the alley for a long time. First, at Finley's word, she had gone to the Sidewinder Saloon and peered inside, holding one of the swinging doors ajar. But Little Owl was not in there. Nor was he in the Silver Hall Saloon, sitting, as he usually did, at a corner table with a stein of beer in front of him.

And he was not anywhere along the boardwalks. Often, when he had drunk so much that he could not get back to the wickiup, he would curl up on a bench along the walk. She would find him there and help him onto the back of their pony. The horse she would not let him take from the wickiup because she knew that he would only sell it for drink money.

And what an endless anguish it was in her woman's heart to have her husband, mute and without fire, allow her to forbid him anything. In his younger days, when they had lived among their own people, he would have beaten her if she dared to withhold anything from him. He would have flung her to the ground and shouted at her in a fury, *I am the head of our family and no squaw will tell me what to do or not to do!*

It was the measure of his fall that he no longer offered to beat or strike her, no longer contested her words at any time. He only grunted and shook or nodded his head and shambled toward Picture City for drink. Yes, it was an evilly distorted world they lived in now.

She did not see Little Owl at first when she entered the alley. She did not believe that she would find him there, but she knew that she must look in every place before she dared return to Finley and ask for his help. What if he asked her—Did you look in such a place?—and she had to answer, in truth—No, I did not. No, she must try all the places before she—

Then she saw her husband lying in the mud.

It was two things at once to her; first, an icy constriction in her bowels and stomach, a thumping pressure at her temples. Yet, at the same time, almost a relief because the sight of him there was proof that the omen had been true and that some values in their life, at least, remained as they should.

It was not until she bent over him, however, that she knew his death and the hideousness of it.

A sound of animal pain tore the lips drawn back from her teeth, and with a sharp intake of breath, she scuttled backward. In her haste, she slipped and fell. Scrambling to her feet again, she started running, all the black horrors in her world pursuing her.

By the time she reached Finley's office, she could hardly breathe. Wheezing, she fell against the door, clubbing weakly at the glass.

Finley had to catch her when he opened the door.

"*What?*" he asked her in Apache.

She could not speak. Only sobbing gasps escaped her lips as she pointed down the street.

Hastily, Finley ran over to the stove and pulled his boots on. Then, grabbing his jacket off the clothes tree, he hurried outside, feeling the clutch of the woman's hand on his sleeve as they started along the walk. Behind them, he heard the fall of Boutelle's following boots.

She would not go up the alley again. She stood pressed against the side of the bank, shivering impotently as Finley and Boutelle walked in to where the body lay. Finley squatted down and turned Little Owl onto his back, his hand sliding underneath the Apache's buckskin shirt.

"Dead," he murmured.

"Is it one of those two men?" asked Boutelle.

Finley didn't answer. Reaching into his shirt pocket, he took out his match case. Opening it, he struck a match and lit the wick of the tiny candle inserted in the case. Then, roofing the flame with his palm, he held it close to Little Owl's face.

*"Good God."* Boutelle's voice was faint.

If ever a look of heart-wrenched terror had been imprinted on a man's face, it was on Little Owl's. The dark features were stiff with it; the mud-caked lips drawn back frozenly in a hideous grin of fright, the dark eyes open wide and staring. It took an effort for Finley to force down the lids of those horror-stricken eyes.

"What in God's name happened to him?" a sickened Boutelle asked.

Again, Finley didn't answer. He ran the candle flame along the length of the Apache's body, looking for a wound. As he did, the tight pain in his eyes began changing.

"There's not a mark on him," he said quietly. The very quietness of his voice seemed to underline the words.

"His heart then," said Boutelle. It sounded less like a statement than an uneasy question.

"I don't know," said Finley.

Letting the rain douse the candle, he shut the cover of the match case and slid it back into his shirt pocket. Then, raising Little Owl to a limp, sitting position, he lifted the dead Indian across his shoulder.

It was remarkable how light he was, Finley could not help thinking. It was as if once the weight of self-respect had gone from Little Owl, his body had complied with the loss, grown fragile and honeycombed with the weightlessness of defeat. Some men, in loss, grow heavy, thought Finley. Some merely wasted away like Little Owl.

He didn't notice where the eyes of Little Owl's wife were looking as he passed her. If he had noticed and thought about it, he would have guessed that her gaze was averted because she was afraid to look upon death until the actual moment of bodily preparation.

He was unaware of the fact that she had seen the tall, broad form standing in the shadows across the street from them. He was unaware that the stricture around her heart was so close to that stricture which had killed her husband that she, herself, almost lost the power to breathe and stand and almost went pitching forward into the mud.

Darkness wavered behind the woman's eyes. Horror sucked at her breath, licked across her brain with a cold, rasping tongue. Only the greatest exertion of will kept her on her feet. With a drawn-in gasp of air, she pushed away from the bank and followed Boutelle closely. She must not look at the tall, dark figure, she knew. He must not realize that she knew of his presence. If she died now, then all was lost.

Back inside the office, Finley lowered the body to the bench beside the door and covered it with his slicker. The expression on Little Owl's face, as it was hidden away, fused itself into Finley's consciousness like a brand seared into flesh.

"I'll take him to your—" he began to say in Apache before he realized that Little Owl's wife was not there.

He looked over at Boutelle. "Where did she go?" he asked.

"I didn't see," the younger man answered. He couldn't take his eyes off the covered figure on the bench.

"Wasn't she with us?"

Boutelle swallowed. "I thought so."

Finley went over to the door and opened it. Stepping out onto the walk, he looked toward the south end of town but saw nothing. Grunting, he went back inside and closed the door. He walked across the office and entered the small hallway that led to the back door. He found the door slightly ajar. She had gone this way then. But why? She should have stayed and gone with the body when Finley took it to her wickiup for burial preparation.

Shaking his head, Finley closed the back door firmly and turned. And this had started out, in the words of Appleface Kelly, as a "gala day." Well, it had, very early, turned into something far different.

"Why did she leave?" asked Boutelle.

"Apache dread of death," said Finley, not wanting Boutelle to know any more than he did.

"What do you suppose happened to him?" Boutelle asked.

"I don't know," said Finley.

He would, most certainly, not answer that question. Boutelle had shown no desire to understand the Indians' point of view. It would do little good for him to tell Boutelle that, as far as he could see, Little Owl had been frightened to death.

She had run, hobbling, all the way to the tethered horse, then walked the horse far out of Picture City. Only there, breathless, a stitch knifing at her side, had she dared to mount and gallop to the wickiup.

She stayed there only long enough to wake her eldest girl and tell her to watch over the other children until her mother returned. She did not tell the girl that Little Owl was dead. There would be time enough for that in the morning.

Right now there was a ride to be made.

Quitting the wickiup hastily, the Apache woman mounted the pony and kicked at its bony sides. The old animal surged forward underneath her, its thin legs driving at the muddy earth. Little Owl's wife set her teeth and braced herself for the ride.

It was a long way to the camp of Braided Feather.

# THURSDAY

# Six

THE TWO OF them were in Corcoran's Gunsmith Shop. Al Corcoran was pulling down a rifle from the wall rack. No, Al, pleaded Finley, you're *wrong*. Al Corcoran didn't say a word. He began to load the rifle. Finley knew that he was going to go after Braided Feather and shoot him. Don't be a fool! he said. If you do that, you'll start the whole thing over again! The treaty won't be worth the paper it's written on. Corcoran said nothing. Al! cried Finley. He jerked the rifle out of Corcoran's hands and threw it on the floor.

Corcoran went over to the wall rack and took down another rifle. For God's sake, Al! said Finley. He tore the rifle out of Corcoran's grip and flung it on the floor. Corcoran drew the pistol from his holster. Al, don't, said Finley. Corcoran squeezed the trigger, and Finley felt a bullet club him on the chest. He fell back against the workbench. Corcoran was walking toward the door, the smoking pistol in his hand. The next one is for Braided Feather, he said. No, it isn't, Finley said vengefully. He drew his pistol out and tried to fire it, but the trigger stuck. When he jerked it desperately, it broke off against his finger like brittle glass. Oh, God! moaned Finley. He lunged for one of the rifles on the floor.

Before Corcoran could get out the door, Finley fired three bullets into his back. Al flung forward onto his face, and Finley staggered to his feet. You won't break my treaty now, he said. I won't let you. He fired another bullet into Corcoran's body.

Then, outside, there was a thundering of hooves. Braided Feather and his men came galloping toward the front of the shop. Finley ran out to tell them that the treaty was safe, but as they galloped up, they threw two torn and bleeding bodies at him. Suddenly, Finley knew he had been wrong. No! he cried. No! I can't be wrong!

Finley jolted in his bed. He sat up, gasping.

Outside and down the street there was a rising thunder of hoofbeats. For a second, Finley sat dazed, staring at the window with sleep-drugged eyes. Then, with a brusque motion, he flung aside the covers and dropped his legs to the floor. He stood and raced across the carpet to the window and jerked up its shade.

It was barely light. Main Street stood empty in the gray of morning. But the thunder was coming closer, and Finley turned his head to the left. Instantly, his mouth dropped open in dumb astonishment.

Galloping into town were approximately three dozen Apache braves.

Finley gaped down at the street with eyes that could not believe what they saw. He looked for the leader of the party and saw, with added shock, that it was Braided Feather. He stared down blankly as the Apache chief went rushing by, the hooves of his horse casting up gouts of mud.

Then, whirling abruptly, he raced to the bed and jerked his nightshirt off. He was dressed in twenty seconds, his arms and legs a blur of agitated motion. Jerking on his boots, he jumped up and sprinted to the door, snatching his hat from the bureau as he passed it. The door went crashing against the wall as he flung it open and sped into the hallway.

He met Boutelle as he half-skidded across the second-floor landing, his hand squeaking on the bannister. The younger man, a long coat thrown over his nightshirt, feet thrust bare into his boots, looked at Finley angrily.

"So much for your treaty!" he snapped.

Finley didn't take the time to answer. Darting past Boutelle, he descended the stairs in a series of step-engulfing leaps. Boutelle followed hurriedly.

"What's wrong, Mr. Finley?"

Finley shot a glance to one side as he raced across the dim lobby. He saw Mrs. Vance in her nightgown standing in the doorway to her and Mr. Vance's apartment.

"Don't know, ma'am!" Finley answered breathlessly. He jolted to a halt before the door and jerked it open, the bell tinkling sharply.

"Is it an attack?" cried Mrs. Vance.

"No!" he shouted over his shoulder as he plunged into the chilly morning air. Turning right, he began to run again along the plank walk. Down the street, the Apaches had drawn their ponies up in front of the general store. At first, Finley didn't see what they were looking at.

Then he caught sight of the man sitting there on the general store's porch.

Within earshot now, Finley skidded to a halt in time to hear Braided Feather address the man in Apache. The agent stopped so abruptly that Boutelle, running close behind, almost rammed into him.

Across the street, the man remained seated, his eyes on Braided Feather as the chief spoke.

"What did the Indian say?" Boutelle whispered, not recognizing Braided Feather.

"He asked the man what he wants," Finley translated hastily, his gaze fixed on the seated man. Who was he? Finley wondered. Why had Braided Feather ridden all the way to Picture City just to see him?

As Finley wondered, the man stood slowly and moved to the edge of the walk. The agent noticed how the Apaches seemed to cringe at his approach, how the ponies nickered in restless alarm and tried to back off.

The man answered Braided Feather.

"What did he say?" whispered Boutelle.

Finley's face had grown suddenly taut. He did not seem to have heard the question.

"What did he *say*?" Boutelle repeated angrily.

"He wants to know where the Night Doctor is."

*"Who?"*

The Indian agent waved him off and leaned forward, listening intently as Braided Feather spoke again. He heard a sound in the chief's voice he had never heard before—the sound of fear. It made him shudder.

"We do not know," Braided Feather was telling the man, edging his horse back slowly as he spoke. *"We do not know."*

The man smiled coldly.

"It does not matter," he said. "I will find him."

Suddenly, Braided Feather jerked his horse around and drove heels to its flanks. In an instant, the other Apaches followed his lead and the street was shaking with the impact of driving hooves.

"Wait!" Finley shouted to the chief. But if Braided Feather heard, he gave no sign of it. Face a carven mask, eyes held straight ahead, he drove his horse toward the edge of town. In a minute, every Apache was gone.

Finley stood for a few moments, staring in the direction they had gone. Then, slowly, his gaze shifted to the man.

"What in the name of heaven is going on?" demanded an angry, confused Boutelle.

Finley shook his head, looking at the man.

"Are those the Apaches we met with yesterday?"

"Yes."

"Are they trying to—"

"Hey, what in hell's going on around here?"

The two of them turned as Appleface Kelly came stomping up, wearing a long, gray overcoat over his nightshirt. His eyes were puffy with sleep, and there was a growth of dark stubble on his cheeks. In his hands he carried a rifle.

"I thought there was a treaty with them bastards," he said.

"There is," said Finley. "This has nothing to do with the treaty. They rode in to see him." He gestured toward the man across the street.

Appleface squinted at the man. "Him again," he said.

"You've seen him before?" asked Finley.

Appleface told him what had happened at the Sidewinder Saloon the night before.

"He asked for Dodge?" said Finley. This thing was getting beyond him.

"That's what Eddie Harkness figgered he wanted," said Appleface. He glanced across the street. "Wonder who in hell he is anyway," he said.

"Maybe we'd better find out," said Finley.

"I would like to—" Boutelle began, then stopped as the Indian agent stepped away.

"Watch y'self," Kelly muttered after him.

Finley nodded once as he started across the muddy street toward the man, who, apparently oblivious to the agent's approach, had gone back to the chair and was looking toward the hotel again.

Finley stepped up onto the walk.

"Good morning," he said.

He was not prepared for the sudden tightening that took place in his stomach muscles when the man's eyes turned to his. It took an effort of will to keep his voice from faltering.

"My name is Finley," he said, trying to sound casually affable. "I'm the Indian agent for this territory."

The man looked at him without answering.

"You—speak English?" asked Finley. Kelly had said that he did, but there seemed to be no reception in the man's face. He eyed Finley without blinking, his face as still as a rock.

"If I can help you in any way . . ." Finley went on, talking more from instinct than design. "I know the Indians who just spoke to you and—"

There was a sudden glittering in the man's eyes which made him stop.

"You know the Night Doctor?" asked the man.

Finley felt a chill lace through the muscles of his back. The way the man had asked it, almost hungrily.

"I know of him," said Finley.

"*Where is he*?" asked the man.

Finley realized in that instant that he would not have told the man where the Night Doctor was even if he knew. He had no reason for this except a feeling in his gut.

"I don't know that," he said.

The man turned away, no longer interested in Finley. Why does he want to see the Night Doctor? the agent wondered.

He was about to say something about knowing Professor Dodge when the man raised his head a little to see who it was that was riding into town down beyond the hotel. And Finley saw the scar.

He couldn't take his eyes off it. They were still fixed to the discolored line of tissue when the man turned and looked at him.

Finley drew in a quick breath and forced his eyes up.

"I'm sorry," he said.

Looking into the man's eyes was like staring into two black pits.

"That must have been . . . quite a cut," Finley heard himself saying.

The man's brutally appraising look altered. Abruptly, almost terribly, he was smiling, but it was not a smile that bore warmth for Finley or for anyone.

"Someone cut my head off once," he said.

Finley shuddered. "Really?" he said, but the bantering tone he tried to put in his voice failed completely.

He stood looking into the man's black eyes for another moment. Then, without another word, he turned and stepped down off the walk. He knew he had learned nothing, that if anything he had been made a fool of. Yet he also knew that he'd had to get away from the man, that he couldn't have stood there by him for another second.

Reaching Boutelle and Kelly, he turned right and started back for the hotel. The two men fell into step beside him.

"What'd he say?" asked Appleface.

"Nothing," said Finley. He didn't want to talk about it.

"Who is he?" asked Boutelle. "And why did the Apaches ride here to see him?"

"I don't know," Finley said tensely. "He told me nothing."

"You think there's gonna be trouble with the Injuns?" Kelly asked.

"If they'd come in to make trouble," Finley told him, "they could have wiped us out. You know that."

Appleface grunted. "That's so." His step faltered. "Well . . . I better get me some clothes on before I get arrested. I'll see ya later."

"All right." Finley kept walking determinedly toward the hotel, trying to rid himself of the cold and frightened restlessness in his gut. He'd never felt like this in his life, and he neither liked nor understood it.

Kelly fell out of step and turned away from them. As he walked back to his boardinghouse he kept glancing across the street to where the man sat. Who in the hell is he, Kelly wondered, that Braided Feather should come riding all the way into town just to see him?

"The man told you absolutely nothing?" Boutelle asked after Kelly had left them.

"Only that he wants to see the Night Doctor," Finley said, hoping this would satisfy the younger man.

"Who in God's name is the Night Doctor?" asked Boutelle.

"An Apache shaman," Finley answered. "A medicine man," he added as Boutelle started to say something. "He was a member of Braided Feather's tribe."

"Was?"

Finley grunted, glancing back over his shoulder. The man still sat in the same position, looking up at the hotel. Finley traced the line of his gaze and saw that it ended on the second story—perhaps on the window of Professor Dodge's room, it occurred to him. Although how the man knew where Dodge's room was, was another question added to the rest.

"Is he dead?" asked Boutelle.

Finley started. "What?"

"The Night Doctor," Boutelle said acidly. "Is he dead?"

"I don't know," said Finley.

"Why did he leave his tribe?"

"He didn't leave it; he was driven out," Finley answered. "Braided Feather outlawed him."

"Why?"

Finley pushed open the hotel door and started in.

"For tampering," he said.

"What do you—"

Boutelle stopped. The Vances were in the lobby, turning from one of the windows where they had been watching. Realizing the state of his dress, Boutelle headed directly for the stairs. After he was dressed, he'd confront Finley again and this time, by heaven, the agent had better give straight answers and stop this nonsense about any Night Doctor. If Finley thought for one second that he could condone the Apaches' obvious disinclination to abide by the conditions of the treaty—not the least of which was the clearly stated rule that they were to keep away from Picture City—he had another think coming. And on the day after the meeting, too! Good God, did Finley think him an idiot?

Finley, at that moment, was thinking of anything but Boutelle's mental capacity.

"No, it wasn't a war party," he was assuring Mrs. Vance. "They were here to see a man. Which is what I want to—"

"Yes, we saw," said Mrs. Vance. "He's the same one who came here last night."

Quickly, she told Finley about the previous night. As she described the open window and the footprints ending in front of it, the agent stared at her almost blankly.

"You think he . . . went *out* the window?" he asked.

"I don't see what else he could have done," she said.

"That scar, did you see that scar on his neck?" added Harry Vance.

Finley nodded, feeling as if he were involved in some ridiculous dream and not actually standing in the hotel lobby talking to the Vances.

"Tell me," he said, "did he happen to mention *why* he wanted to see Professor Dodge?"

"No, he didn't," Harry said. "Just went upstairs and . . ." He shrugged weakly.

Finley shook his head and grinned wryly. "Sure makes a lot of sense, doesn't it?"

"It makes no sense at all," said Mrs. Vance, as if he were speaking seriously.

"You say you don't know when Professor Dodge is coming back?" Finley asked Harry.

"No, he didn't say," said Harry. "Never does."

"I see. Well, when he does come in, will you tell him I want to see him right away? Before that . . . other fellow gets to him."

"Yes, sir, I'll do that," Harry said.

"Good."

Except that things were far from good, Finley thought as he went up to his room to shave. He kept trying to put the bizarre details into some kind of pattern, but they wouldn't fit together. How could you connect such shapeless pieces as a stranger who might or might not be an Indian; a stranger who wanted to see an outlawed medicine man and a professor of archaeology; a stranger with a jagged scar around his neck ("*Someone cut my head off once*") whose presence gave one a sense of sickened dread; a story about this man jumping from a second-story window without injury; and Braided Feather, a fearless Apache chief, riding in to see the man, then fleeing as if devils pursued him? These things made no overall sense—or, if they did, the sense was lost to Finley.

He was just relocking his door when it occurred to him that there might be two more details to be added, details which would make the pattern, should it emerge, even darker.

The death of Little Owl. And the disappearance of Tom and Jim Corcoran.

# Seven

AT EIGHT O'CLOCK that morning, Al Corcoran rode into Picture City with the corpses of his brothers.

He did not look to either side of the street, did not note the shocked faces of the people who came out from their stores and houses as he passed. He did not notice the man sitting on the porch of the general store. He rode on woodenly, eyes staring and glassy, mouth set into an ugly, lipless gash, gloved hands curled tightly round the rein ends of his mount.

Following behind on a lead walked the horse that had belonged to his brother Tom. The two bodies lay across its back, covered by a frayed blanket. They had been put there, faces down, their arms and legs hanging loosely, the wrists and ankles tied together. One of the men was barefoot, the feet pale white and gnarled with dark blue veins. Across the wrists of the other was a darkened spiderweb of dry blood. The two bodies stirred with the motion of the horse as if they were trying to move.

Corcoran rode directly to the Indian agent's office before reining up. Slowly dismounting, he wrapped the reins of his horse around the hitching post and, ignoring the stares of the people around him, strode to the plank walk, stepped up onto it, and went to the office door. He did not go in. Turning the knob, he shoved the door open as hard as he could.

Inside, Finley and Boutelle looked up in shock as the door crashed against the wall.

"*Al . . .*" Finley's voice was startled.

Corcoran did not reply. He stared in at the agent, gloved hands fisted at his sides. Finley pushed up from his desk and hurried to the door. Corcoran didn't move, blocking his way. Finley stopped in front of him and looked over the heavy man's shoulder. There was a tightening on his cheeks as he saw the bodies.

"Where were they?" he asked.

"Out where the Injuns were," muttered Corcoran.

Finley blinked. Then, as Corcoran stepped back, he moved out onto the walk, eyes stark with pain. This was the moment he had dreaded most since yesterday. Abruptly, a fragment of his dream flared briefly in consciousness: him coming out of some building, seeing the two bleeding bodies. He shuddered and stepped down off the walk into the mud. Corcoran followed him.

Finley stood beside the second horse, his hand closed around a cold, white ankle. He felt sick with premonition. These two, still bodies could plunge everyone in Picture City into a bloody nightmare again.

"Now tell me it wasn't Injuns," Corcoran said between his teeth. "*Tell* me, Finley."

Finley drew in a fast breath of the cold, morning air. "Al—" he started.

With a sob of fury, Corcoran tore the blanket away.

"*Tell me it wasn't Injuns!*" he cried.

Across the street a woman moaned softly and had to be supported. On the walk, Boutelle gagged and caught onto one of the columns that supported the balcony overhead.

"*Oh, my God,*" Finley murmured.

One of them was naked, his blood-drained body raked with deep, blue-edged gullies, half his chest torn away. The other, the one who had been Jim Corcoran, had no face—only a blood-oozing mask of shredded meat. Here an eye was missing, there an ear. Gouges deep enough to lay the hand in sideways had been slashed across backs and bellies. Nerve and artery ends hung like black ribbons. In one thigh, bone showed. From the half-missing chest, rib ends stuck out jaggedly, their ivory darkened by blood.

Finley could not speak or draw his eyes from the butchered remains. He felt his heart thumping slowly and heavily in his chest. Horror swept over him in waves that seemed to blot away the sane world which he had managed to cling to until this moment.

He hardly felt the hand on his arm as Corcoran turned him. He stared blankly at the trembling, wild-eyed man.

"You get them soldiers," Corcoran muttered hoarsely. "You get them right away. You hear me?"

Sucking in breath, Finley disengaged Corcoran's shaking fingers and picked up the blanket lying on the mud. Carefully, he laid it back across the two bodies and closed his eyes for a moment, trying to force back into himself the strength he needed.

Then he turned back and took Corcoran's arm.

"Come inside," he said.

Corcoran jerked his arm away. "I'm takin' them to Packer's," he said.

"Al, we—"

The heavyset man turned away, moving almost drunkenly. He stopped in mid-step and looked back over his shoulder.

"I'm comin' back here in a couple o' minutes," he said. "If you ain't ready t'go for the soldiers by then, I'll go after them murderin' bastards myself."

"I'll be here, Al."

Corcoran untwisted the reins of his horse and started walking it away. Behind, the second horse lurched forward, the two bodies twitching at the abrupt movement. Finley stared at the arms and legs as they began to hitch and sway.

He wanted to call after Corcoran, but his voice would not function. He knew he should go with the nerve-shattered man, but he needed a little time to get hold of himself. He stood, wordless, watching Corcoran move away toward Packer's Funeral Parlor.

*It wasn't Braided Feather.* That was the only thought his mind could manage. Yet what good would it do to say that to Corcoran now? What dissuasion could it possibly be to a man who had found his two brothers in that hideous state and, with his own hands, put them on horseback? By any judgment of sanity, he should ride immediately to Fort Apache and get the soldiers, send them after Braided Feather's tribe.

Finley shuddered. That was the crux of it, he realized. This *wasn't* sanity. It was all a maniac's dream. No Indian had done that to the Corcoran brothers. Only a giant animal could have torn them so. Was that possible? Finley thought suddenly.

No. It was that man. Behind all sensible thoughts, the secret place of his mind knew that somehow that man was responsible. But how? The conscious mind could not imagine an answer. How could one man do what had been done to those two, husky young men?

There was only one course he could think of in the midst of all this, to ride to Braided Feather's camp immediately—or to the reservation if they had already reported there—and find out who the man was and why the Apaches feared him. He'd take Corcoran along. He didn't dare leave the grief-maddened man to himself. He had planned to wait for Professor Dodge's return, but there was no time for waiting now; that was frighteningly clear. Something had to be done immediately.

Boutelle followed him back into the office—a paler, far less steady man than had left it minutes before.

"And you defend them," he said, his voice thickened by the horror he had just witnessed.

"No Indian did that," was all that Finley could think of saying.

"Then what did, Mr. Finley?" demanded Boutelle.

Finley sank down heavily on the bench where Little Owl had lain the night before. He'd taken the body to its wickiup an hour earlier. Yes—what did? his mind repeated. And what had made the old Apache die without a single mark on him?

"I don't know, Mr. Boutelle," he answered. "I only wish I did." He exhaled slowly. "I only know it wasn't Braided Feather's—"

"Finley, you're blind!" cried Boutelle. "Or mad—or worse!"

At any other time, Finley would have lost his temper at such vitriolic, accusing words. Yet now, off balance, he only looked up defenselessly at the younger man's infuriated expression.

"Are you going to the fort?" challenged Boutelle.

Finley rubbed a hand across his dry lips. What answer could he give that would not brand him as brainlessly submissive?

He could only shake his head, not in answer so much as in reflection of his perplexity.

"I see," said Boutelle, and for a second, Finley almost envied the simple clarity with which the younger man saw the situation, devoid of complications, of perilous possibilities.

"Then I'll ride there myself with Mr. Corcoran," said Boutelle. "I shall have dispatched a—"

*"You will not."* Anger came at least strongly enough to stiffen Finley's words and make him stand abruptly. "Now you listen to—"

He grabbed Boutelle's arms as the younger man started turning and twisted him back. "I said *listen*!" he snapped.

"If you think—"

"There's more involved here—"

"Get your hands off me!"

"—than just a senseless Indian murder!" Finley drowned him out. "Use your brains! What possible good could Braided Feather have gotten out of murdering two of our citizens on the very day he agreed to a peace treaty with us! After ten years of constant battle! No! I say, no! It wasn't Indians!"

"And I say only an Indian could do what was done to those men!" Boutelle lashed back. "I say only an Indian could *conceive* of it!"

"You don't—"

"I'm riding to that fort, Mr. Finley!" the younger man yelled. "With you—or without you!"

"*You are not*!" roared Finley, his hands tightening so hard on the younger man's arms that Boutelle winced. "I'm the authorized agent for this territory and until I'm replaced, it's my decision to make! And I say there'll be no soldiers yet!"

Boutelle's repression of fury was easily visible. Finley could almost see him swallow it.

"Very well," the younger man said in a tight, quiet voice. "Very well, Mr. Finley. You are quite correct. Your authority supersedes mine."

He paused, looking at the agent with cold contempt.

"At least for now," he said.

Spinning on his heel, he moved for the door. Finley started to say something, then changed his mind. Let him go, he thought. Maybe righteous indignation would keep him occupied for a while, the preparation of damning reports to Washington.

Well, there was no time to waste in concerns about Boutelle. Grabbing his hat and jacket, he stepped outside.

"Oh, Jimmy," he called to a young boy passing by.

"Yes, sir." Jimmy Taylor came over to him.

"Like to earn a short bit?"

"Yes, sir."

"I'm expecting Al Corcoran back here any second," Finley told the boy. "Will you tell him that I'm going to the hotel for a minute, then I'm going to the livery stable for my horse."

"Yes, sir."

Finley pressed the coin into the palm of the boy's hand. "Tell him to wait right here, Jimmy. Tell him I'll be right back. You understand?"

Jimmy nodded. "Yes, sir, I understand."

"Good." Finley patted his shoulder and turned away. What if Dodge came back while he was gone? the thought occurred. He'd better tell Harry Vance to tell the professor to stay in his room until he got back.

Blowing out breath, Finley stepped off hurriedly, wondering how in God's name he was going to talk Al Corcoran into going in peace to the Apache camp.

Al Corcoran came out of Packer's Funeral Parlor and started walking the horses down the street. He was going back to Finley's office now and Finley had better have his mind made up.

Corcoran shivered fitfully, still feeling sick. He was sure that he would never forget the experience of carrying his brothers into Packer's back room. He could still smell that raw-meat odor of them in his nostrils, still see in his tortured mind their torn flesh and protruding bones as he lay them down on the tables in the dim, chemical-reeking room.

He sucked in raspingly at the air. The Apaches would pay for this, by God. One way or another, he'd get out to Braided Feather's camp for revenge—even if he had to go alone with a high-powered, telescopic lens rifle. There would be payment in full, he swore that to himself and to the memory of his brothers.

He was thinking that when he saw the man.

At first it failed to strike him. He walked on past the store, his mind too deeply intent on thoughts of vengeance to notice the evidence before his eyes. Then, abruptly, he stopped and looked back so quickly that it drove sharp twinges of pain up his neck.

The man was wearing Tom's clothes.

For a moment, Corcoran couldn't move. The enormity of it seemed to paralyze his muscles. He stood, immobile, his eyes fixed on the tall stranger who sat on the porch of the general store, looking toward the hotel.

Then the fury came, breaking Corcoran loose from his paralysis, moving through his veins like a current of acid. Slowly, mechanically, he walked across the street and tied his lead horse to the post.

He took a deep, trembling breath and unbuttoned his jacket, pushing the right side of it back with his hand. For a moment, he rested the curve of his hand on his pistol butt.

Then, lowering his hand, he stepped up to the edge of the walk.

"You," he said.

The man's gaze turned and lowered to the murderous eyes of Al Corcoran.

"Where did you get those clothes?" Corcoran asked slowly. He shuddered at the sight of this savage-looking man, but forged ahead.

The man was silent, his dark eyes perusing Corcoran's face.

"You hear me?"

The man's lips curled upward slightly in a scornful smile.

"I do not understand you," he said in Apache.

Corcoran shuddered with animal hatred. "An *Injun*," he whispered through his teeth so softly that only he could hear it.

Abruptly, he reached back and slipped the Colt from its holster. The man's gaze dropped to the barrel end pointed at his chest.

"What are you doing?" he asked in Apache. There was no alarm in his voice.

"Get on that horse," said Corcoran, gesturing with his head. He felt his finger tightening on the trigger and willfully loosened it.

A man came out of the store and stopped in his tracks at the sight of Corcoran's drawn pistol. Corcoran noticed him from the corners of his eyes.

"Get back inside," he said.

"I do not understand you," the stranger said, as if Corcoran had spoken to him.

Corcoran's chest heaved with shaking breath. Jerkily, he moved back a pace and gestured toward the second horse with his pistol barrel. He emphasized the movement by a loud cocking of the Colt's hammer.

The man still did not look disturbed. He glanced over at the hotel, then, without a word, pushed to his feet. Stepping down off the walk, he released the reins of the second horse and mounted it with a single, fluid motion. There he sat waiting while Al pulled his own horse free and mounted it hastily.

"All right," said Al, "now *get*." With the pistol barrel, he pointed toward the north end of town.

The man drew his horse around and started walking it down the street. Behind him, pistol held across his saddle, rode Corcoran. This was one Apache Finley wasn't going to save, he was thinking. Finley wasn't even going to know about it. Maybe the agent was right about it not being Braided Feather, but he was wrong about it not being an Indian—because, right there ahead of him, tall and steady on his horse, rode the Indian who had killed his brothers. The one who was going to die in the same way they had.

"Hurry it up, will you, Sam?" asked Finley.

"Yes, sir, Mr. Finley." The old man dropped the saddle across the mare's twitching back and started working on the straps.

Finley stood impatiently on the straw-littered floor of the stable. His fingers flexed restlessly inside his gloves as he sighed deeply. Yesterday, about this time, he had been in the Bluebell Restaurant with Boutelle, having his steak and eggs. The day had looked promising.

How much could change in twenty-four hours.

He glanced toward the old man and saw that he was almost finished now. Moving to the horse, he rechecked the straps hastily, then nodded. "That's fine, Sam." Raising his boot to the stirrup, he lifted himself to the saddle quickly.

"See you," he muttered and nudged his boot heels against the mare's flanks. Its shoes clattered noisily across the stable floor, then squished into the mud outside. Finley reined it left and rode down the street to his office.

Jimmy was still there, leaning against one of the balcony columns. As Finley drew up, the boy straightened and came over to the edge of the walk.

"Hasn't he come back yet?" Finley frowned.

"No, sir."

"You're positive you couldn't have missed him?"

"Yes, sir, Mr. Finley. I never caught sight of him."

"I see." Finley clenched his teeth. "Well, thank you, Jimmy." Pulling the mare around, he heeled it into a quick canter down the street.

A minute later he was rushing out of Packer's front door, his face a mask of alarm. Was Al already taking things into his own hands? Had he ridden to Fort Apache by himself or with Boutelle? Or worse armed himself and started off for Braided Feather's camp? The agent looked around indecisively, the fist of one hand hitting at his leg. Good God, was there to be no end to this insanity?

He was riding past the store when he saw that the man was no longer there. Reining up quickly, he dismounted and jogged inside.

"Mr. Casey, did you see where that strange man went?" he asked.

He didn't expect the answer he got.

Corcoran rode behind the man, his .44 leveled at the broad back. Every few seconds he had to consciously restrain himself from squeezing the trigger and sending a bullet into the stranger's body.

He didn't want to do that yet. He wanted to save that for last. First, he wanted to make the man beg for his life, to cry for mercy. Or, failing that (these damned Injuns sometimes died without a sound) he wanted, at least, to kill him slowly, inch by inch. Not with one merciful shot.

Corcoran pressed his teeth together and shivered. He had never wanted to kill so much as he did now. His eyes glittered as he stared at the man ahead. Damned butcher, he thought. The Indian must have sneaked up on his brothers from behind. This had been no face-to-face attack, that was for certain. His brothers had been strong, husky boys. No one Indian, no matter how strong, could have done what had been done to them unless . . .

Corcoran's breath hissed out between his lips. Damned murdering bastard! he thought. When I'm through with you, they not only won't know who you were, they won't know *what* you were.

Raised in his stirrups, Finley galloped out of Picture City, eyes scanning the meadow for Corcoran and the man. He had to find them now, before . . .

He grimaced painfully. Before what? his mind demanded. There was no answer. Only vivid memories of a dead, staring Indian so terrified that his heart had stopped and of two hideously mutilated bodies. Only premonitions of a horror that went far beyond all fears men came to live with and accept.

Corcoran tightened his reins and pulled the bit back in his horse's mouth.

"Stop," he said.

Ahead, the man, without glancing back, pulled in his horse and halted it. They were in a small, tree-ringed glade that slanted down gradually toward a narrow, rushing stream. It was a place hidden to anyone but those within a range of several yards. Corcoran didn't want anyone to stop this play.

The man sat motionless on his horse as Corcoran dismounted. The heavyset man walked slowly across the ground and raised his pistol.

"Get down," he ordered.

The man raised his leg backward over the horse's body and settled easily to the ground. It drove a fiery bolt of rage through Corcoran to see the pant leg of his brother hitch up across the boot top.

"Raise your hands," he said.

The man raised his arms, his expression one of unconcern. Corcoran stiffened, a tight, venomous smile forming on his lips.

"I thought you didn't savvy me," he said.

Was that a smile? Beneath his glove, the fingers that held the Colt went white across the knuckles.

"I understand," the man said calmly.

With a savage cry, Corcoran jumped forward and slammed the pistol barrel across the man's skull.

Without a sound, the man staggered back a few paces, then caught his balance. As he straightened up, the raised collar of the jacket he wore slid down, revealing the livid scar. The sight of it jolted Corcoran, but not enough to drive away the murderous fury in him.

"You son of a bitch, Injun scum," he said in a soft, tense voice. "I'm gonna cut you into meat."

The man stood erect again, seemingly oblivious to the trickle of blood across his forehead.

"Wipe that filthy smile off your—"

Corcoran broke off suddenly and smiled crazily himself.

"No, go ahead," he said through his teeth. "Smile, you Injun bastard. That's how they'll find your head—*smilin'*." He looked down at the scar. "That's gonna make me a perfect line for cuttin'."

A chuckle sounded deeply in the man's chest.

"Go on, laugh, you bastard!" said Corcoran, his voice breaking.

The man did laugh. Eyes glowing with a savage amusement, his lips flared back, his laughter rocking terribly in the air. Hatred boiled up behind Corcoran's eyes. With a deranged sob, he pulled the trigger and fired a bullet into the man's chest.

• • •

Finley jerked the mare around and looked in all directions. Dear Christ, was he too late already?

In the distance, a second shot rang out and echoed off the hills.

Corcoran stood frozenly, staring at the man. His mouth hung open; a line of spittle ran across his jaw.

The man stood smiling at him.

Corcoran fired again, instinctively.

The man twitched back a little but did not fall. A hollow sound of disbelief stirred in Corcoran's throat.

"Who are you?" he asked, but the words came out only as a jumble of brainless sounds.

The man took a step toward him.

"No." Corcoran edged back, his eyes wide with terror.

The man kept coming. With a sobbing gasp, Corcoran fired again, and again. He kept pulling the trigger even when there was only the click of the hammer on empty chambers.

"All gone," said the man.

Corcoran cried out hoarsely as he backed against the tree. He pressed against the gnarled trunk tightly, shaking his head in tiny, fitful jerks, his eyes bright and staring.

"*Who are you*?" he gasped.

The man stopped a few paces away.

"*Look*," he said, and he stretched out his arms.

Corcoran recoiled against the tree, the beginning of a scream strangled in his throat. He stood there for a moment looking at the man with eyes that had lost their sanity. Then his vibrating legs gave way, and he slid down to a half-sitting position on the tree roots, looking up stupidly at the man and what the man was becoming.

When the monstrous shadow fell across him, he tried to scream, but there was no strength in him. Mouth yawning open in a soundless shriek, he went limp against the tree. He barely heard the inhuman screech that filled his ears.

A trembling Finley pulled up his horse.

He didn't want to enter that glade. A moment before, Corcoran's two horses had come bursting out of it and passed him, their eyes mad with terror. He wanted to turn and follow their frenzied gallop across the meadow. The scream still seemed to ring in his ears—a sound the like of which he had never heard in all his life.

Only after a long while could he force the shuddering mare to enter the glade.

It seemed to be deserted. No tall figure stood there waiting for him; there was no sign of Al Corcoran. Finley sat stiffly on the fidgeting horse, his eyes moving over the silence of the glade.

Then he saw the pieces.

# Eight

THIRTY MINUTES BEFORE he saw the low line of Picture City's buildings in the distance, Professor Albert Dodge knew in a flash of angry revelation that he was going back to Connecticut.

He'd had enough, more than enough. Odd that it took this last abortive foray into the hills to make him realize it. God knew the disenchantment had been mounting for at least a year. Perhaps this last, frustrating trip was a disguised blessing.

Under the circumstances, he wasn't sure who was more of an idiot—"Appleface" Kelly or himself for believing Kelly. "Oh, yes, sir, Perfessor. There is sure as hell some broken pots out there, some bones, too." Dodge could hear the man's assured voice repeated in his memory. "Moron," he muttered. He'd soon discovered that the pot shards were dry clay formations and the bones leftovers from wild animal kills.

Then it had begun to rain.

Rain? he thought irascibly. More like horseback riding underneath a waterfall. In less than twenty seconds he'd been drenched. No shelter at first. He'd tried to stop beneath the overhang of a piñon tree. That had been a waste of time. After several minutes of that, he'd been forced to move on, the rain alternately coming straight down on top of him or blowing into his face with the violence of buckets of water flung at him by some deranged antagonist.

On top of that, his horse had slipped and fallen.

By the time he'd located the small cave, he was dripping wet and screaming vehement curses at Kelly, the sky, the land, life itself.

The cave helped precious little. He'd crawled into it nonetheless, over still-moist animal droppings and the remains of small, partially devoured creatures he could not identify.

There he had cowered, while the rain poured down, at last falling into a sluggish sleep despite his dread that some wild animal—a coyote, a cougar—might clamber into the cave and attack him. It would have been a fitting conclusion to Kelly's Folly, he thought. To be ripped asunder by some ravenous beast.

All he'd gleaned from this infernal little outing was a fallen horse, a bruised side, a chilled body, and mud-caked clothes where he'd fallen from the horse. He was lucky, he supposed, that he didn't have a broken leg or worse; the damned, skittish animal could have landed square on top of him.

No, he was going back; that was suddenly, definitively settled. Back to Fairfax College if they'd have him. What a fool he'd been to leave there in the first place, and for what? Heat, wind, dust, rain, snow, the company of fools and no archaeological results worth a tinker's damn.

Unless one counted that single, bizarre experience. Dodge shuddered. Would he never be able to shake it from his mind? Well, that was not surprising. He was, as a matter of fact, astounded at himself for not having left the territory immediately after it had taken place.

Except, of course, that it had taken no more than a month for logic to refute the apparent evidence of his senses. Really, it couldn't have happened as he recalled. Something in the drink the shaman had given him. For protection, the old man had cautioned. Perhaps something in the fire smoke he'd been compelled to inhale throughout the ceremony. Even—it was not inconceivable—that the shaman had placed him into some involuntary state of mental control.

But certainly—*certainly*—he could not have actually seen what he thought he saw.

If only I had a pick, a shovel, Finley had kept thinking.

What he'd been compelled to do was torturous and ghastly. He'd seen victims of Indian raids in the past, seen a village of Apaches slaughtered by the cavalry.

He'd never seen anything remotely like this.

He didn't want to dispose of the pieces but knew he had no choice. If anyone from Picture City—or God forbid from Fort Apache—saw what had happened here, there would be no doubt whatever in their minds that Braided Feather's tribe had violated the treaty with a massacre.

He might not have even known it was Al Corcoran if it hadn't been for the head lying yards distant from the mangled body parts, as though it had been hurled aside in some maniacal rage.

The look on Al Corcoran's blood-streaked face was virtually a duplicate of the one on Little Owl's face—an expression of total, unutterable horror.

Finley had kept his eyes averted as he'd reached down until he felt Al Corcoran's hair. Then gingerly, grimacing, sickened as he did it, he'd picked up the ripped-off head and carried it back to where the dismembered body lay.

He'd hoped, for several minutes, that the rain had been severe enough to soften the earth so that he could dig a shallow trench with his knife and hands. But scant inches below the muddy surface, the earth was, as always, brick hard, making that impossible.

He'd been forced to gather together the shredded, torn remains and cover them as best he could with large stones and small boulders. Throughout, he'd tried to look at something else, anything else but the hideously butchered leavings of what an hour earlier had been a man.

It was not always possible. Jarring sights kept stinging at his eyes and brain. Corcoran's left hand and wrist dangling purplish veins and arteries. His right arm, the hand clutched into a rigid, white fist. His left leg almost pulled loose. The trunk of his body, chest and belly, ripped apart as though by the claws of a raging bear; his internal organs strewn across the blood-soaked ground.

He tried not to think about what might have done this to Corcoran. He knew only that it wasn't any of Braided Feather's people.

But what it had been was something he could not address at the moment. It was enough to cover over Al Corcoran's torn and mutilated form.

He could not allow himself to visualize what sort of being was capable of such horrible savagery.

As Dodge rode into Picture City, a bitterly ironic memory struck his mind. Him ranting to the Fairfax Board of Governors that archaeology was supposed to be a living science, not some musty, dry-as-bones collection of facts dredged up in classrooms.

"Oh, yes," he muttered sourly. Well, he'd be happy to return to musty fact collections just as soon as stagecoach and train could get him back to civilization.

He looked down at himself as the horse clopped slowly toward the hotel. Never had he looked more pitiful. By God, he'd have these damn clothes burned before he left town. But first a bath, sleep, and then a decent meal with copious whiskey as a side dish.

Then—*hallelujah*—to the stagecoach office to reserve a seat on the morning coach to White River and all parts east. Back to genteel, sensible surroundings.

"Amen," he muttered.

He left the horse at the livery stable. Thank God he'd only rented the use of it. Selling it could take forever.

"Looks like you took a tumble," the man at the stable said with a grin.

Dodge only grunted and turned away, feeling a slight sense of pleasure that he'd never bothered to learn the man's name.

The journey along the plank walk to the hotel made him wince. His stockings were still damp inside his boots, and his mud-stiffened trousers rubbed against the skin on his legs; the long coat, still wet, weighed him down oppressively.

"So *there* you are, Perfessor," Harry Vance said as Dodge entered the lobby. "You been out all night?"

"Obviously," Dodge answered curtly. "My key, please."

Harry slid the key from its slot and handed it over. "Lots of excitement here this morning," he said.

"Oh?" Dodge turned for the staircase.

"Yes, sir. Ol' Braided Feather and a passel of his braves come riding in."

Dodge stopped and looked around. "Why?" he asked.

"Seems they come to see this man," Harry answered.

"They came in to see a *man*?" Dodge sounded dubious.

"*Some man* though," Harry said. "Matter o' fact, he come in here last night lookin' for you."

Dodge felt a slight chill waver through his body. "Me?" he asked.

"Yes, sir. Asked for you by name. Weird-lookin' duck he was."

Dodge swallowed; his throat felt suddenly dry. "Why, what did he look like?" he asked. He felt as though somebody else had asked the question.

"Well, he was powerful tall," Harry said. "I mean *powerful* tall, mayhaps six foot five inches."

"Yes?" Dodge asked, barely audible.

"He looked sort of like an Injun, but I don't think he was," Harry said. "Had a"—he gestured vaguely at his neck—"big . . . thick . . . *scar* around his neck, *all* around it. Awful-lookin' sight."

No, thought Dodge. He thought he heard a faint voice speak the word aloud in his ears. No, it wasn't possible.

"Told him you wasn't here," Harry said, wondering about the blank stare on Professor Dodge's face. "He went upstairs anyway. That was peculiar, too. He had mud on his boots and tracked it on the carpet in the upstairs hall. But the tracks, they stopped by the window at the end of the hall. The window was open and the man was gone. We thought maybe he'd gone in your room so we took a look, 'scuse that. He wasn't there though. So he must have jumped from the window. From the second floor though?"

Dodge felt as if he were about to faint. His head felt very light and there was a buzzing in his ears. No, this is wrong, he thought. It wasn't happening. It couldn't be.

"Where—" He coughed weakly. "Where is he now?" he asked. He was appalled at how weak and strained his voice had become.

"Ain't seen him since this morning when the Apaches rode in to see him," Harry said. "You know who he is?"

His voice trailed off on the last two words of his question because Professor Dodge had turned away and moved abruptly toward the stairs. Doesn't look too steady, Harry thought. He watched the professor start up the steps, holding tightly to the bannister. Was it his imagination or had the blood drained from Dodge's face? He certainly looked disturbed enough. Who *was* that weird duck anyway? He'd have to tell Ethel about this right off.

Dodge heard the thump of his boots on the steps but could barely feel his feet. He seemed to have gone numb all over. He kept shaking his head with tiny, jerking movements. There had to be another explanation for this. It could not possibly be what it seemed.

He twitched in shock as a sob broke in his throat. "No," he whispered.

He half-ran, half-walked down the hallway, unlocked the door to his room and pushed inside. Closing the door quickly, he relocked it, his hand so palsied by fear that he could barely manage it.

Then he stumbled to the bed and dropped down on it heavily. He felt completely drained of strength. He had not felt such a sense of dread since that night in the shaman's wickiup when . . .

*"No!"* He drove a fist down weakly on the bed. It couldn't be! It was impossible!

*Impossible.*

When Finley got back to town, he left his horse at the livery stable and started toward the hotel. He wanted more than anything to strip away his clothes and take a hot bath, he felt so befouled by what he'd had to do. He could still smell the sickening odor of Al Corcoran's mutilated flesh.

It was when he was taking his key from Harry that he asked offhandedly if Professor Dodge had come back yet.

"Yes, he has," Harry told him. "Just got back about"—he checked the wall clock—"oh, fifteen, twenty minutes ago."

"And he's in his room?" Finley asked.

"Far as I know," Harry answered. "Leastwise, haven't seen him leave."

"What's the number of his room?" Finley asked.

"Twenny-nine."

"Thanks," Finley said, turning away.

The bath would have to wait, he thought. Dodge was the only one who might be able to shed some light on this unnerving situation. He couldn't imagine why that grisly-looking man would want to see Dodge, but at least it was a start—and all he had to go on at the moment.

Reaching the second floor, he walked to the end of the hall and knocked on the door to Room Twenty-nine. He twitched his head a little to the left, thinking he heard a gasp inside the room. Then there was dead silence. He waited for Dodge to open the door.

When nothing happened, he knocked again, a little more loudly.

There was no response. Could Harry have been wrong? he thought. Had Dodge gone out again?

He knocked once more and said, "Professor Dodge?"

There was no answer. "Are you in there?" he asked loudly.

Silence. He grunted in frustration and started to turn away.

"Who is it?" he heard Dodge ask from inside the room, his voice tight and barely audible.

"Billjohn Finley," he answered.

"Who?" The question sounded faintly.

"Finley." He grimaced with irritation. "The Indian agent."

Silence again. Now what? Finley wondered. Was the man going to let him in or not?

"What do you want?" Dodge asked. There was no mistaking it now; what he heard was the voice of a frightened man.

"I'd like to talk with you," Finley said, trying to keep the aggravation out of his voice.

"What about?" Dodge demanded.

For Christ's sake, Finley thought. What the hell is wrong with the man?

Then he thought of everything that had happened since yesterday. If Dodge was part of it, it was not surprising that he'd sound disturbed.

"I want to talk to you about that man," Finley said, somehow knowing that Dodge would know exactly what he meant.

Silence. What was Dodge doing? he wondered. And was he actually going to open the door?

"Are you alone?" Dodge's thin voice drifted through the door.

"Yes," Finley answered.

Another few seconds passed. Then Finley heard the door being unlocked. It didn't open. "Come in," Dodge said.

Finley opened the door and stopped short.

Dodge was pointing a derringer at his chest.

Finley's hands flew up, palms spread. "For God's sake," he said.

The professor lowered the derringer. "Come in, come in," he said. As Finley did, Dodge shut the door quickly and relocked it. That lock wouldn't do much good if that man chose to break the door open, Finley thought.

Then he was looking at Dodge's face, knowing in an instant that the professor was very much a part of the strange events which had taken place. The small man's expression, while not as exaggerated by shock, very much reminded him of the look on Little Owl's face. The look on Al Corcoran's face.

The look of a man confronted by total, overpowering terror.

# Nine

FINLEY GLANCED TOWARD the bed. Dodge had thrown two suitcases across the mattress and begun to pack them—if flinging articles of clothing into them with clumsy haste could be defined as packing. More evidence, he thought. Not that he needed it now. Dodge's appearance and manner made it more than apparent that he was getting ready to flee.

"Leaving?" he asked.

The professor's Adam's apple bobbed convulsively. "What do you want?" he asked.

"I think you know what I want," Finley told him.

"I have no idea—"

"I want to know who that man is," Finley broke in. "I want to know why he wants to see you. Why he asked about the Night Doctor. I want to know why Braided Feather and his braves rode all the way in from Pinal Spring to see him. I want you to tell me what's going on, Professor."

"I have no idea—" Dodge started again.

"I think you do," Finley interrupted angrily. "The man asked for you in the Sidewinder Saloon. Then he came here and asked for you. He—"

"I don't know who he is!" Dodge cried. He turned away abruptly. "Now if you'll please go, I have packing to do."

"I don't think you can run away from him," Finley told him quietly. "Four men are dead already and—"

He broke off at the look of stunned dismay on Dodge's face. "What?" the professor murmured.

"Four men have been killed," Finley said. "One of them was frightened to death. The other three were torn apart by God knows what. Now, I know—"

He broke off a second time as Dodge began to shake, making faint whimpering sounds in his throat as he stared at Finley.

The agent felt a burst of pity for the little man. "For God's sake, Professor," he said. "*What is going on?*"

He couldn't tell at first what Dodge was saying, his voice was so weak and trembling. Then he heard the words, repeated and repeated. "I can't, I can't, I can't."

"Why?" Finley stared at him, feeling as though he were involved in some bewildering nightmare.

He drew back a little involuntarily as Dodge moved toward him. He felt the small man's shaking hand clutch at his arm. "Please," Dodge said. "*Please.* Take me into custody."

"What?"

"Arrest me. Lock me in the jail," Dodge begged.

"Professor, I'm the local Indian agent, I'm not the—"

"Take me to Fort Apache then," Dodge interrupted. His eyes were brimming tears now. "Hand me over to the cavalry."

"Professor, you are going to have to tell me what is going on."

"I *can't*!" Dodge cried in agony. "There isn't time! I have to be protected or—"

He stopped abruptly.

"Or?" Finley said.

"Please take me with you," Dodge said. "When I'm safe, I'll tell you what it is, I promise you."

"It would help if you told me now, Profess—"

"No! It wouldn't! There isn't time!" The little man was weeping now. Finley felt the sense of dark alarm within him growing. Who in God's name was that man that he could cause such blind terror in everyone he encountered?

As he led the professor out through the front door of the hotel, he started in surprise as Dodge jerked back with a hiss, pulling his arm free and shrinking back into the doorway.

"What is it?" Finley asked.

Dodge couldn't speak. He made a faint noise of dread as he stared out at the street. Finley looked in that direction and winced.

Across the street, the man was just dismounting from one of the Corcoran horses. But they had galloped off, Finley thought in confusion. How did the man . . . ?

"What are we going to do?" Dodge whispered, terrified.

Finley drew in a deep, restoring breath. He wasn't going to let this thing completely spook him, he resolved. He simply wasn't.

"We are going to walk to my office, Professor," he said as calmly as he could. "Then we are going to the stable, get two horses, and ride out of town to Fort Apache."

He wondered if Dodge had heard a single word he'd said. The little man could not remove his stricken gaze from the man across the street. Finley looked in that direction. The man was just sitting down in the chair again to watch the hotel.

"Come on," Finley said, taking hold of Dodge's arm.

"*No.*" The little man hitched back in blind alarm.

Finley grimaced with anger. "Professor, I'm going down to my office now. Come with me or stay here alone."

Dodge looked at him in a sudden panic. "Don't leave me," he begged.

"Then come with me," Finley said. "I'm not going to stay."

He stepped off, glancing back. Dodge hadn't budged. He was still gaping at the man across the street. Again, Finley looked in that direction. An icy shiver ran up his back.

The man was looking toward the hotel doorway. Could he see Dodge? Finley wondered.

He looked back at Dodge, who still stood frozen just inside the hotel doorway.

"Professor," he said, "the street is filled with people. The man isn't going to go after you with all these people around."

He glanced around. There weren't that many, he saw. He wasn't going to tell Dodge that, however. "Come on," he said, "I'm going now."

"Wait," Dodge pleaded pathetically.

He came out slowly, pretending that he didn't know the man was across the street. Finley glanced aside, stiffening as he saw the man rise suddenly. Jesus, was he going to approach Dodge anyway?

He grabbed the professor's arm and started leading him toward the office.

"Just walk smoothly," he said. He had to force himself not to glance across the street. Not that he'd know what to do if the man was crossing toward them. Confront him? Run?

"Is he coming for us?" Dodge asked in a faint voice.

Finley almost glanced aside despite his resolution not to do it. He clenched his teeth and looked ahead determinedly. "Just walk," he said.

He could feel the rigid tension in Dodge's arm as they moved down the street, their boots thumping on the plank walk. Finley couldn't help himself from glancing at the window of Chasen's Dry Goods. He saw the man reflected, still across the street, watching them. What did that mean?

he wondered. That he'd changed his mind about seeing Dodge? That he wouldn't accost Dodge unless the professor was alone? He couldn't help wondering what the man thought of him for leading Dodge along the street.

He had his answer when they reached the office. As he opened the door and ushered Dodge inside, he could not prevent himself from looking toward the man.

He shivered as he saw that the man had moved along the opposite side of the street. Already, he was standing almost directly across from the office.

The look he directed at Finley chilled the agent's blood.

It was a look of murderous hostility.

Swallowing with effort, Finley went inside and shut the door with a cowed sense that there was probably no door that could shut away the man if the man chose to enter.

As he turned toward the office, he was startled to see Boutelle across the floor from him, standing with Barney Gans, who ran a small horse ranch somewhere in the vicinity of Pinal Spring.

From the look of him, Barney had been riding hard, his long coat splattered with mud, streaks and specks of it across his face and hat, on his hands.

"What's going on?" Finley asked.

Boutelle glanced questioningly at Dodge.

"This is Professor Dodge," Finley told him. "I'm taking him to Fort Apache."

"Good." Boutelle's voice was grim. "I'll go with you."

Now what? Finley thought.

"Tell Mr. Finley," Boutelle said to Gans.

"It's the Injuns, Mr. Finley," Barney said. "Braided Feather's band. They left their camp and took off for the mountains."

Oh, Christ, Finley thought. He wasn't prepared for this. "You're sure?" was all he could think to say.

"Yes, sir. I was bringin' in some strays and saw them movin' off."

"Are you satisfied now?" Boutelle demanded. "Is this enough? Can we tell Colonel Bishop that—"

"Listen—" Finley interrupted, then broke off instantly and turned to Dodge. "Can you tell us something to explain this?" he asked. "Mr. Boutelle is convinced that Braided Feather's band is behind all this. I think you know differently. Now will you please tell Mr. Boutelle what's actually going on?"

Dodge gulped. "I can't," he murmured. "I have to leave."

"Professor, *we have got to know*," Finley said irritably. "Mr. Boutelle—"

"Mr. Boutelle is convinced that this is one more dereliction on the part of the Apaches," Boutelle broke in. "One more indication of their utter contempt for the agreement they signed only yesterday!"

Finley grabbed Dodge's arm. "Damn it," he said. "Tell us who that man is and why he wants to talk to you, and to the Night Doctor."

Dodge began to shake, tears rising in his eyes again. "I can't," he said. Boutelle looked at him, wondering how Dodge fitted into any of this. He was convinced it was the Apaches. Still . . .

"Barney, thank you for riding in and telling us this," Finley said to Gans. "I'm going to find Braided Feather and his people and ask them what this is all about."

"You don't think—" Barney began.

"You're going to *talk* to the Apaches?" Boutelle said incredulously. "You're still not going to call in the troops to—"

"Barney, I'll be in touch with you later." Finley said, cutting off Boutelle. "Thank you again."

"That's okay, Mr. Finley," Barney said.

When he'd gone, Finley turned back to Boutelle. The young man's face was set into a grim expression. I cannot believe how much has gone wrong in the past twenty-four hours, Finley thought. He glanced at the wall clock. Jesus. It hadn't even been twenty-four hours yet.

Bracing himself, he spoke to Boutelle.

"You don't know everything that's going on here," he said. He threw a resentful glance at Dodge. "And it doesn't look as if you're going to right away—any more than I am."

He gestured brusquely toward the bench by the door. "Wait there," he told Dodge. Despite the small man's continuing dread, Finley was losing patience with him. Dodge might conceivably solve this problem with a simple explanation. He couldn't imagine what that explanation might be, but if it was there, Dodge damn well owed it to them.

"I know what you believe, Mr. Boutelle," he said. "I know it makes sense to you. But I'm convinced there's more involved here than a broken treaty."

"*A broken treaty*?" Boutelle said coldly. "Have you already forgotten about those two butchered men?"

"No, I haven't forgotten about them," Finley said, noticing the frightened look Dodge was giving Boutelle. He almost told Boutelle about Al Corcoran, then decided against it; there simply wasn't time.

"I'm going after Braided Feather," he continued. "I have to hear his side of the story before I can decide what to do. I'm sorry, but that's the way it's got to be for now."

Boutelle stared at him in silence. Finley heard the wall clock ticking and saw, from the left side of his vision, the brass pendulum arcing back and forth.

"I see," Boutelle finally replied.

Finley turned away and moved to the cupboard to get his saddlebags and supplies.

"I'll go rent a horse," Boutelle said.

Finley turned in surprise. Boutelle was heading for the door.

"You're going with me?" Finley asked.

Boutelle stopped and looked around.

"Is there any reason that I can't?" he challenged.

Finley thought about it for a moment. "No," he said. "Glad to have your company."

"That I doubt," Boutelle murmured, moving to the door again and opening it. "I'll meet you at the livery stable," he said.

Finley watched Boutelle close the door. He was impressed. It would never have occurred to him that Boutelle would volunteer for such a trip.

He grunted with dark amusement as he turned back to the cupboard. Glad to have his company? he thought. Boutelle was right. He doubted it, too. At least he'd know where Boutelle was, though. That would prevent the younger man from riding to Fort Apache on his own and reporting Braided Feather's flight to Colonel Bishop.

A look of concern tightened his face again. Why *did* Braided Feather take his entire band away from their camp? He'd never known the chief to evidence a moment's cowardice in the past. Now he was taking flight with all his people.

Something was driving them away. Something which obviously terrified them.

He looked at Dodge.

The little man was standing by the window, pressed against the wall, peering around its edge.

"Is he still there?" Finley asked.

His voice made the little man twitch and look toward Finley with a gasp.

"Is he?" Finley said.

Dodge drew in a shaking breath. "Yes," he said, his voice thin. "You *are* going to take me to Fort Apache, aren't you?"

"No," Finley answered.

Dodge looked at him in shock. "You're *not*?" he said.

"Why should I take you anywhere?" Finley demanded. "You're not willing to help me. Why should I help you?"

"Please," Dodge said. "I can't tell you."

"Then go by yourself," Finley snapped.

"Damn you, don't you have the slightest idea of what we're all involved in here!" Dodge cried, startling Finley. "If you knew what that man really is!"

"What is he?" Finley demanded.

"*Something you don't want to know about*," Dodge told him. "If you had the brains you were born with, you'd leave the territory with me and never come back!"

Finley looked intently at the little man. Clearly, Dodge was overwhelmed by dread.

He sighed. No use, he thought. He wasn't going to get anything helpful from the professor. He may as well forego the hope.

"You can go with me," he told the professor. "But I can't take you to Fort Apache."

"But you *have* to," Dodge said in a panicked voice.

"It's in the opposite direction from the way I have to go," Finley told him. "I'm sorry. You know what I have to do."

"You can't just leave me," Dodge said pleadingly.

"I'm sorry," Finley said, gathering supplies together. "I'll stay with you as far as I can. Then I've got to head into the mountains." He looked over at Dodge. "Maybe you want to come with me, see Braided Feather yourself."

Dodge said no more. He stood by the window in silence, peering out at the man.

The next time Finley looked at him, the little man was slumped on the bench, bending over, holding his head in his hands. Finley had never seen a more defeated-looking man. He felt sorry for Dodge again.

But there was nothing more he could do about it.

# Ten

AS THEY RODE down Main Street, headed for the south end of town, they had to ride past the hotel. Across from it, sitting in the chair again, was the man. Seeing him there, it occurred to Finley that ordinarily if short-tempered Elbert Zweig, who owned the grain shop, saw anyone sitting in his chair, he'd charge out and roust him. That there was not a sign of Zweig made it obvious that he had no intention of confronting the man.

He glanced at Dodge. The professor was staring straight ahead, face set into a rigid mask.

Finley glanced at the man in the chair, shuddering as he saw that look again directed at him.

He felt a tightening of reactive anger. Damn the man anyway, he thought. If the Marshal had been around, Finley could have told him that the man had stolen one of the Corcorans' horses; that would be enough to get him thrown in jail.

But could the jail even contain the man, Finley wondered, remembering that glade and the sight of Al Corcoran torn apart like the prey of some wild animal. The last time he'd seen a living thing so mangled was when he'd stumbled onto a hawk devouring a rabbit it had just caught. His startling of the bird had made it rush up suddenly into the air, scattering the bloody fragments of flesh in all directions.

"You really think that man is involved with what's happening?" Boutelle's voice made him start.

Finley glanced at the man in the chair to see if he'd overheard. If he had, he gave no indication of it.

"Ask the professor," he answered.

Boutelle looked at Dodge. "Professor?" he asked. If the small man knew something about this situation, Boutelle could not fathom why he was so reluctant to reveal it.

"Not yet," was all Dodge said, his lips barely moving as though he didn't want the man in the chair to think he was speaking.

Ten minutes later, they were out of Picture City.

After they were gone from sight, the man stood slowly and moved to Al Corcoran's horse. He swung his giant frame onto the saddle and reined the horse's head around.

He would not lose track of the professor this time.

They saw the grayish-white smoke before they were close enough to see what was burning.

"What could that be?" Boutelle asked.

"Unless I'm wrong, it's Little Owl's wickiup," Finley told him.

In several minutes, they could see the burning structure. Because of the heavy rain the day and night before, its hide walls were still damp, smoldering slowly instead of burning quickly as they would have in drier weather.

Little Owl's widow and children had just finished loading a travois with their few belongings. They looked around apprehensively as they heard the approaching hoofbeats. Seeing Finley, Little Owl's wife said something to her children and they became less restive.

Boutelle looked at them with impolite curiosity as they rode closer to the burning wickiup. He had not seen Indian women and children before. His only exposure to the Apaches had been the meeting yesterday and the few minutes in town this morning, and that had only been with Braided Feather, his rancorous son, and whatever braves had come along with them.

Frankly, he was appalled by the sight of Little Owl's widow and children. They looked dirty and diseased to him, their clothes in wretched condition. Did they ever wash? he thought. But even as he thought it, he sensed the injustice of that observation. To live like this was scarcely conducive to cleanliness. Not that they care, I'm sure, he thought.

In light of all that, however, why in the name of God were they burning the one shelter they had, meager and mean though it was?

He asked, and Finley told him that it was because of Little Owl, that it was an Indian practice to burn their dwelling places after a death.

"With his body *inside*?" he asked, repelled.

"It's their way," Finley answered.

Boutelle was silent for a few moments before asking, "Can you find out if she knows anything about the Apaches leaving their camp?"

"She wouldn't know anything about that," Finley replied.

"Ask her about her husband then," Boutelle said. "Maybe he knew—"

"Impossible," Finley interrupted. "From the moment she knew her husband was dead, his name never passed her lips, and in no way whatever will she ever refer to him for the rest of her life."

"Really," Boutelle said, not impressed by the information, merely reacting to it.

They stopped by the smoking, slowly burning wicki-up, and Finley, dismounting, spoke to Little Owl's wife. Boutelle could not help but notice the kindness in his voice when he spoke to her. What did the man see in these people anyway? he thought. Their hideous depredations on the settlers of this territory and beyond would certainly seem to disqualify them from the status of acceptable human beings.

He looked over at Dodge. The professor was clearly unhappy about them stopping at all. He kept looking back toward Picture City, his expression deeply anxious. Did he think that man was going to follow them?

Boutelle tried not to allow himself to be misled by what appeared to be complications in what was going on. The facts were clear enough. The Apaches had signed the treaty in bad faith, promptly massacred those two young men, and now were fleeing from the obvious consequences.

The rest was extraneous. That man—as grotesque as he was to look at—could not conceivably be behind all this. Very well, Professor Dodge was terrified of him. Dodge seemed to be an educated man, but that did not prevent him from being credulous as well. Perhaps he'd done something to offend the man and feared reprisal.

As far as the so-called "Night Doctor" . . . Boutelle made a scoffing noise. He had no intention of succumbing to anything which remotely smacked of mysticism. God knew the man with the scar looked powerful enough to commit any conceivable variety of mayhem without being a mystical being. That the Apaches feared him was not all that peculiar. They were a naive, superstitious lot at best and . . .

His train of thought broke off as Dodge said loudly, "Can't we go?"

Finley looked up at him without expression, then turned back to Little Owl's widow and said a few more things to her. Boutelle saw him pat her gently on the back and smile. Then he returned to his horse and mounted. Without a word, he pulled the mare around and nudged his heels against its flanks, causing it to trot away. Boutelle did the same, then Dodge. The three men rode off from what had been Little Owl's home and now was only a smoking framework of poles and burning hides.

"What did you say to her?" Boutelle asked, riding up beside Finley.

"I wished her luck," Finley muttered.

"You didn't suggest she take her family to the San Carlos Reservation?"

"I wouldn't send a *dog* there," Finley responded.

The bitterness in his voice shut Boutelle up. Obviously Finley was in no frame of mind to be rational, he thought. Let it go. Soon enough, the agent would have to accept the facts and have a troop of cavalry sent in pursuit of the fleeing Apaches.

Dodge followed them, relieved when Finley heeled his mare into a slow gallop. The further away from the man he got and the faster, the better he'd feel.

Finley pulled up his horse and twisted around to look at Dodge.

"This is as far as I can take you," he said. "The fort is that way."

Dodge stared at him blankly. "You're really not going to—"

"You can still come with us," Finley cut him off. "Talk to Braided Feather. Tell him—"

"No," Dodge interrupted.

Finley's lips tightened. "Suit yourself," he said. Boutelle saw him struggling with his anger and controlling it. Then Finley spoke again.

"Listen to me, Professor," he said. "This is your last chance to prevent what could well be a catastrophe. You know a lot more than you've told us. Please . . . *please* don't hold back anymore. *Who is that man?* Why are the

Apaches running from him? Why are *you* running from him? What does the Night Doctor have to do with it? For God's sake, what's that damn *scar* around his neck?"

It seemed as though Dodge was about to speak. His lips stirred soundlessly, his expression tautly anxious.

Abruptly, then, he looked behind them, hissed as though he saw something, and kicked his boot heels at the horse's flanks, galloping off toward the fort.

"I hope he makes it," Finley said after a few moments.

Boutelle didn't know how to respond. Despite his resolve, his mind kept getting cluttered with these complications, all of them leading to one unanswerable question.

What *did* the tall stranger have to do with what was going on?

He watched Dodge galloping away at high speed.

As though pursued by the demons of Hell.

The campground was built beside a running stream within a grove of trees, a thick windbreak of pine, spruce, and piñon.

There were eighty-seven tepees covering a clearing of almost four acres. They surrounded an open area of ground in which stood an oversize tepee which Boutelle took to be a meeting lodge of some kind.

Each tepee was constructed of a tripod of poles tightly covered by buffalo skins, their flesh side outward. All of them looked slightly tilted to Boutelle, which he took to be deliberate.

The camp was deserted.

Boutelle's gaze moved across the quiet area. Several fires were still burning low, their wood embers dark red. Pots hung over them as though the Apaches had not even had the time to remove them. Boutelle could smell some kind of food now burning in them.

His gaze shifted to where an ancient-looking steer was standing, motionless, looking off into the distance.

"Why did they leave it?" he asked.

"Too old, too slow," Finley said. "They didn't want to be held back."

"How do you know that?" Boutelle asked.

Finley didn't answer, and Boutelle had the sudden impression that Finley knew a great deal about these people and their land. For a few moments, he felt alien and helpless, then fought it off. No need for that, he told himself.

"Now what?" he asked.

Finley gazed at him, and Boutelle had the impression that the agent wouldn't hesitate to leave him there if it served his purpose.

"Now we find them," Finley answered.

"Where?"

Was that a scornful smile on Finley's lips? The Indian agent pointed. "Thataway," he said. Boutelle was going to question him regarding how he knew, then realized that to someone with Finley's experience finding tracks would present no difficulty. He decided not to speak.

"If nothing else," Finley said, "this should make it clear to you how frightened these people are. Indians can pack and move very fast, including their tepees. That they've left them here—even left cooking utensils—well . . ." He looked at Boutelle grimly. "You'll have to take my word for it," he said. "Let's get out of here."

He swung up onto his mare and started off. Boutelle swallowed, trying to repress a sense of apprehension.

They were heading for the mountains.

Dodge knew he was driving his horse too hard, but he couldn't help it. He cursed himself for not demanding a different horse from the one he'd ridden on his trip into the hills. He should have a fresh mount, one that could move faster.

He looked down at the horse. Its neck was covered with lather. He should let it slow down; it needed a break. He couldn't allow it though. He kept kicking his boot heels against its flanks and uttering demanding cries for more and more speed. The Appaloosa's legs drove down like pistons against the still wet earth, casting up sprays of mud. Dodge glanced down at himself. He was filthy with the stuff.

Forget it, he told himself. *Forget it.* For the seventy-third time since he'd left Picture City, he looked behind. No sign of the man, he saw. Which didn't mean the man was not pursuing him. He had to guess that Dodge was headed for the fort. It wouldn't even require a guess if he'd spotted the place where Dodge had separated from Finley and Boutelle.

He tried to stand a little in the stirrups to relieve the pounding of his body on the hard saddle. He wished to God he were a better rider. It had never seemed a necessity before.

Now it did.

He looked over his shoulder toward the mountains. Already, they were darkening. For God's sake, what had happened to the day? he thought angrily. He had to reach the fort before sunset. The vision of him being forced to gallop in the dark terrified him.

He reached up his left hand and rubbed it across his sweating neck. Despite the chilly air, he felt hot. He should stop and remove his coat, but he didn't dare take the time. He had to keep going. Until he reached the fort, he was in constant danger.

The horse struggled up a rise, and Dodge reined it to a skidding halt, twisting around on the saddle to look again at—

The sound he uttered in his throat was something between a sob and a cry of fear.

In the distance, riding hard, the man was following him.

"*God*," Dodge whimpered.

He drove his heels into the horse's body, and it lurched forward with a frightening groan. *Don't fail me now*, Dodge thought desperately.

The Appaloosa half-ran, half-slid down the slope on the opposite side, reached level ground and broke into a gallop once more. Dodge caught his breath. Was it his imagination or had the horse just lurched as though the strain was too much for it?

He couldn't even let himself consider the possibility. The horse would get him to the fort. *It had to get him there.* He looked over his shoulder again.

And cried out in despairing shock.

The other horse still followed him.

*But it was riderless.*

*"No!"* Dodge ground his teeth together, kicking wildly at the horse's flanks. He needed a whip, a *whip*! Dear God! *It wasn't possible.*

He looked up at the leaden-colored sky. "No, please," he whimpered. "Please." His heart was pounding violently. His mind kept pleading.

He was looking at the sky again when the Appaloosa's legs collapsed.

Screaming with horror, Dodge was hurled from its back, landing in a twisted heap. Uncontrolled, his frail body tumbled, somersaulting down a rocky slope, the back of his head striking a boulder with violent impact at the bottom.

There was a rushing sound above, a dropping shadow.

Then the man stood at the top of the slope, looking down at Dodge's motionless body.

Ignoring the fleeing Appaloosa, the man moved down

the slope, boots crunching on the layers of small rocks.

At the bottom, he stopped and looked down at Professor Dodge's dead body, his dark eyes filled with hatred for the little man.

Abruptly, then, he leaned over and dragged up Dodge's body with one hand, raised it effortlessly above his head and hurled it away with a snarl of feral rage.

The professor's bruised and bleeding corpse landed more than twenty feet away.

# Eleven

FINLEY LOOKED AROUND at Boutelle and saw the younger man kneading at his right leg. Reining back his mare until he was beside Boutelle, he asked him what was wrong.

"Nothing," Boutelle answered. "I just haven't ridden such a distance in a long time."

Finley looked at the sky. "Well, we should stop soon anyway," he said. "We can't go much further today."

Boutelle frowned. He hadn't planned on spending the night out here.

"Shouldn't we be turning back for help?" he asked. "You really intend to confront the Apaches all by yourself?"

"Better than confronting them with Leicester's troops behind me," Finley said. "That would really be a mistake. Braided Feather wouldn't trust me for a moment if I did that."

Boutelle was inclined to disagree but sensed that it would be a waste of time. Grimacing, he removed his glove and dug the fingers of his right hand into his cramping leg muscles.

"Apaches believe that involuntary muscle spasms are signals of evil events to come," Finley observed. Was that the hint of a smile on his lips? Boutelle wondered. He grunted as Finley moved away from him. Naturally, he didn't believe a word of such nonsense, but after everything that had happened, he would have preferred that Finley kept that bit of Apache lore to himself.

Fifteen minutes later, Finley stopped his mare by the side of a small creek in an aspen grove. The chilling October wind was causing the undersides of the aspen leaves to twist around, making the tree appear as though it was dancing with light.

"Don't get down too close to that brush," Finley told him.

But Boutelle was already dismounting.

He gasped at the sudden buzzing noise beneath him. He felt something thick and soft beneath his boot, then cried out at the fiery sensation in his right calf. He looked down to see a thrash of tan-brown movement in the brush and heard another buzzing sound.

He never knew how Finley got to him so fast. All he knew was that the agent had a long knife in his hand and was stabbing down at something. The buzzing and thrashing increased, and Boutelle saw then what he'd stepped on: a brown and tan rattlesnake at least seven feet long.

"My God," he murmured. Now that the initial shock had passed, the pain in his leg was increasing. I'm going to die, he thought incredulously. Out here. Like this.

He saw that Finley had driven his knife blade through the snake's neck, pinning it to the ground. Pulling a folding knife from a trouser pocket, the agent opened it and started slicing a piece of flesh from the still living snake. The rattler kept striking, but the blade through its neck prevented it from reaching them.

"Quickly," Finley said. He grabbed Boutelle by the arm and half-pulled, half-shoved him to a piece of open ground where he threw him down. He pulled up Boutelle's trouser leg and slapped the piece of rattler flesh on the puncture mark.

Boutelle caught his breath. Despite the pain, he felt a drawing sensation, and in less than a minute, to his amazement, the white snake flesh started turning green.

"Hold it against the wound," Finley told him.

Boutelle did as he was told, and Finley quickly returned to the still thrashing snake and cut another chunk of flesh from its body. Bringing it back, he took the greenish piece of flesh away, threw it aside, and replaced it with the new white piece. Boutelle felt the drawing sensation once more and watched in awe while the second piece of flesh began to change in color as the rattler's venom was sapped from his blood.

Boutelle lay immobile on the ground as Finley kept applying chunks of snake meat to the puncture wound until the flesh ceased turning green. It took almost the entire snake before that happened. It was almost dark by then. Finley had to take out his match case and light the wick of the tiny candle so he could be sure the poison had been totally extracted.

"There you go," he said. "You'll be sore, maybe a little dizzy. But nothing more."

Boutelle swallowed dryly. "Thank you," he murmured.

"My pleasure," Finley said, smiling a little.

"That was a big snake," Boutelle said. "I could have died."

"Easily," Finley agreed.

Boutelle shuddered. "I never heard of treating it that way," he said. "Cutting a crosshatch in the skin and sucking it out, yes, but—"

"That doesn't always work," Finley said. "This way is more certain. Hated to kill the snake, but I had no choice. He bit you, he had to cure you."

"Where—" Boutelle swallowed again, the impact of what he'd just gone through getting to him more and more. He could have died. "Where did you learn to do that?"

Finley chuckled. "From Braided Feather," he answered.

Boutelle had no idea what to reply. Finley grinned at him.

"Bet that leg cramp isn't bothering you now," he said.

While Boutelle rested, Finley unsaddled the horses and tethered them to graze after first letting them drink their fill from the creek.

Then he broke off a pile of aspen twigs and branches for a fire.

"Good wood," he told Boutelle, trying to prevent the younger man from brooding too much about what had happened to him; he knew the danger of that. "Makes a smokeless fire."

Boutelle wondered why it mattered that the fire was smokeless. That man with the scar was interested in Professor Dodge, not them.

"Just as soon no smoke shows," Finley said, as though reading his mind.

When the fire was burning, Finley took supplies from his saddlebags: a slab of bacon, a can of beans, some flour, and a small sack of coffee. "Common doin's," Finley said. "Keep us from starving though."

"You must have known we were out for the night," Boutelle said, trying not to sound accusing.

"I wasn't sure," Finley responded. "I hoped we'd find Braided Feather right away but knew I couldn't count on it." He glanced over at Boutelle. "I'm sorry I can't take you into town to see Doc Reese," he said.

"Do I need to see a doctor?" Boutelle asked uneasily.

"I don't think so," Finley said. "Just thought you might feel better seeing a real sawbones."

"I doubt if he could do any more than you," Boutelle replied. He was still flabbergasted by the memory of what Finley had done. There was no doubt in his mind that he would have died if Finley hadn't acted so immediately.

It made him feel off balance to owe the agent so much. In a matter of seconds, their relationship seemed to have changed completely.

How could he argue with a man who'd saved his life?

"Coffee's ready," Finley said. He poured some into a metal cup and handed it to Boutelle. "Hope it doesn't curl your hair. It's cowboy coffee."

"What's that?" Boutelle asked.

"If a silver dollar floats on top of it, it's done," Finley answered, grinning.

Boutelle managed a smile. Despite Finley's incredible rescue, he still felt achy and a little hot.

"You all right?" Finley asked.

"Considering the alternative, I'd say yes," Boutelle answered.

Finley smiled and sat down with his cup of coffee. "Drink," he said. "If anything can neutralize rattler venom, it's a good, strong cup of Arbuckle's."

Boutelle took a sip, the taste of it widening his eyes. "God," he murmured.

"Little strong?" Finley asked.

"Just a bit," Boutelle sniffed at the coffee, then took another sip and whistled softly. "I may never sleep again," he said.

Finley smiled, then looked serious.

"Listen . . . Boutelle," he said. "All right if I call you David?" he sidetracked himself.

Boutelle hesitated.

"If it bothers you, I won't," Finley told him.

"No, no," Boutelle said. "That's fine." He paused. "Billjohn, is it?"

Finley explained how he got the name. "Both my folks

were satisfied," he said. "At least, they claimed they were. I doubt it, though."

He took a sip of coffee, then removed a cigar case from his inside jacket pocket and held it out. "Want one?" he asked.

"Not right now, thank you," Boutelle answered.

"Understandable." Finley put a cigar between his lips and lit the end of it, drew in deeply, then blew out smoke. "Good," he said.

Boutelle waited. He believed that Finley had been about to say something serious to him a few moments earlier.

"David, do you still think the Apaches are responsible for what's been going on?" Finley asked.

Boutelle felt cornered. Before the rattler bite, he would have responded instantly that of course he did. Now it was a bit more difficult than that.

He elected to do the sort of thing he saw in Washington all the time, the political thing. He reversed the question.

"Do you still think it's that man?" he asked.

Finley's lips stirred in a faint smile, and Boutelle sensed that the agent was aware of what he'd done.

"Look at it this way then," Finley said, confirming the impression. "Does it make sense to you that, on the very day of signing a treaty with the United States—after ten years of war, mind you—Braided Feather would let his braves kill and mutilate the Corcoran brothers—*on their way home from the signing ceremony*?"

Boutelle could not deny that Finley's point was well-taken. Still . . .

"And that, knowing full well that one of the main conditions of the treaty is that they keep their distance from Picture City, he'd ride into town with his braves the very next morning?"

"Well . . ." Boutelle felt his conviction fading.

"They came in to see that man," Finley said. "If they'd come as hostiles, they could have wiped us out at that time of morning. You know that."

"I don't," Boutelle said. "I'll take your word on it, though."

"You do admit they were afraid of that man and left within seconds of seeing him?"

"I . . . suppose," Boutelle had to admit, albeit reluctantly.

"David," Finley said. Boutelle tensed a little at the admonishing tone in Finley's voice; that he did not appreciate. "These aren't dime-novel Indians. These are bone-seasoned Apache warriors. Believe me, there is very little in this world that frightens them. But that man frightens them."

Boutelle nodded slightly. "Well, he certainly seems to frighten Professor Dodge," he said.

"Terrifies him, David," Finley said. "Terrifies him."

He hesitated, then said, "I'll tell you something. He kind o' scares the bejesus out of me as well."

He told Boutelle about his rejected inclination to await the marshal's return and try to put the man in jail for horse stealing. "Not to mention murder," he finished.

Then he told Boutelle about finding Al Corcoran's butchered remains.

"I've seen victims of Apache raids," he said. "They did some pretty god-awful things. But nothing like that."

"Which has been my point—" Boutelle almost said "Billjohn," then couldn't make himself do it. "The Apaches— the Indians—are well-known for their atrocities. You can't deny that."

"I don't deny it," Finley said. "I'm just saying that these atrocities go way beyond what I've seen them do."

"Then how could that man be responsible?" Boutelle

challenged. "How could any one man be responsible for these things?"

"I don't know," Finley murmured. He added something in such a low voice that Boutelle couldn't hear it.

"What?" he asked. It made him uneasy to see how obviously Finley swallowed.

"I said, if he *is* a man," the agent said.

Boutelle felt himself shudder involuntarily. "What do you—" He cleared his throat. "What do you mean?"

Finley didn't answer at first. All Boutelle could hear was the crackle of the low fire and sounds in the night, birds and animals. He stared at the agent's face, firelight reflected on it.

Finley looked away, troubled.

Finally, the agent sighed and tossed his cigar into the fire.

"I'm thinking of the look on Little Owl's face," he said. "You saw it. If ever a man died of fright, it was him."

He hesitated, then continued. "I saw the same look on Al Corcoran's face when I . . . picked up his head," he told Boutelle, who winced at his words.

"You saw the look on Tom Corcoran's face. It was the same look—absolute horror."

He drew in a deep, laboring breath and released it slowly.

"I imagine we'd have seen the same look on Jim Corcoran's face, too," he said, "if his face hadn't been ripped off."

Boutelle winced again. More and more, he was losing confidence in what he'd been convinced of earlier. He tried to believe that it was because of the darkness, the sounds, and the firelight glinting on Finley's harrowed expression. But it wouldn't wash. The Indian agent was right. There were too many abnormal factors in this situation to ignore.

"I'm thinking about the Night Doctor. I'm wondering why that man is so anxious to see a discredited shaman, a medicine man who was banished from his tribe for performing ceremonies he wasn't supposed to perform."

They sat in silence, Finley staring gravely into the fire, Boutelle watching him with a sense of deep disquiet.

"You know," Finley said after a while, "back East, it's civilized and all the mysteries have been dispelled by that civilization. Out here, it's easier to believe that there's still a lot of unexplored ground. A lot of secrets."

He paused again, then added quietly, "I'm thinking of that thick scar around the man's entire neck. When I mentioned it, he smiled at me and said that someone had once cut off his head."

Boutelle wished desperately now that he could speak up and refute the agent's increasingly alarming words. He couldn't, though.

He started as he heard a horrible screeching noise in the distance, looked quickly at Finley. The other man had not responded to the sound.

"What was that?" Boutelle had to ask.

"Owl killing something," Finley said. "Or a hawk." He shrugged. "Maybe an eagle."

# FRIDAY

# Twelve

WHILE THEY WERE riding the next day, heading toward the mountains, Finley following signs Boutelle couldn't see, they began to talk about Indians.

In the daylight—there was even an occasional glow of sunshine to warm the cold air—Boutelle regained some of his confidence in past convictions. The soreness from the rattler bite was almost gone as well, and uncharitable though it was, with little to remind him physically of what Finley had done, it was easier to retrieve beliefs he'd held for so many years.

"About these Plains Indians," he began.

"David, there was no such thing until the Spanish brought in horses."

"And the Indians stole them," Boutelle countered.

"Or traded for them," Finley said. "They were farmers and hunters until they got the horses."

"I was under the impression that the Apache nation—" Boutelle started.

"There *is* no Apache nation," Finley cut him off. "There are only clans and kinship groupings.

"For that matter, isn't it stupid that we call them Indians at all? What if Columbus had thought he'd landed in Turkey instead of India? Would we call them turkeys?"

"Mr. . . . Billjohn," Boutelle said, grimacing slightly. "What do you want to call them?"

"People," Finley said. "That's what they call themselves.

How about the first Americans? They were here before we were."

Boutelle sighed. "I hear your Rutgers background speaking now," he said.

They rode in silence for a while. Then Boutelle spoke again.

"You admitted last night that the Apaches have done some god-awful things," he started.

"And we've done some god-awful things to them," Finley said.

He is really in a bellicose frame of mind today, Boutelle thought.

"As I heard a man in White River say to a companion," he prodded Finley, "*haul in your horns*. By which—"

He broke off as Finley snickered. Clearly, the agent knew exactly what he meant.

"You're right," Finley said. "I'm sorry. I'll try to speak my piece without rattling my tail.

"It's a little difficult for me, though. I was a history major at Rutgers—American history. I wrote my Master's thesis on the Indian situation."

Boutelle was surprised. He'd had no idea the man was that well educated. He felt a twinge of guilt.

"You think the problem started only ten or twenty years ago?" Finley continued. "Indians were living on the East Coast more than forty years ago. Living in peace with their neighbors. In log cabins. Wearing homespun clothing. The Cherokees, the Chickasaws, the Choctaws, Creeks, and Seminoles. They were called the Five Civilized Tribes. Their leaders could read and write English. Their people intermarried with the whites.

"Then Andrew Jackson decided that they didn't belong there. So he had Congress pass legislation to move the Indians to 'an ample district west of the Mississippi.' "

His tone was bitter as he quoted.

"It took nine years to get it done, but by God they got it done," he went on. "Sixty thousand Indians rounded up at gunpoint and marched west under military guard.

"Only fourteen thousand of them survived it."

He smiled and shook his head; it was a smile devoid of humor. "Eventually, the land they'd been given was taken away from them."

He grunted. "That's the way it worked from the start," he said. "We gave them land—that was already theirs, of course. Then when we wanted that land for building or mining or farming or grazing, we took it back and gave them other land further out. Until the land they were given was so bad they decided to fight back. At which point, we began calling them savages."

Boutelle felt as though he should say something to refute what Finley had told him. He couldn't, though. He couldn't think of anything to say.

"I've been an Indian agent for seven years, David," Finley continued. "My job has been to issue supplies and annuities to the Apaches. Annuities that never arrived on time. Supplies that got sold or stolen before they reached me.

"I'm supposed to tell the Indians how nice their lives will be on reservations like the one at San Carlos, which is a malaria-ridden hellhole.

"Of course, no matter what I do, it's hopeless. The Apaches are finished. All the Indians are finished. They got in our way. We wanted their land so we took it. Their days are written on the sand. You and I may not live to see it, but it's going to happen, it's inevitable."

He sighed and smiled bitterly. "Listen, if you think I've got diarrhea of the jawbone, just tell me so. I have a tendency to run on for a day and a half when I talk about the Indians."

They rode in silence for a long while before Boutelle felt compelled to speak.

"Listen . . . Billjohn," he said, "I've lived an isolated life. My family has a lot of money and it made existence very easy for me. I rode, I hunted, I hiked. I traveled the world. Graduated from the best schools.

"My father got me an appointment in the Department of the Interior. I thought I was equipped to handle it. Like so many people back East, I thought I understood the Indian situation perfectly. I read the newspapers, read the dispatches. You're right; I thought of them as savages. I probably still feel that way deep inside. But you've given me a lot to think about I never had before, and I thank you for it."

Finley's smile was broad and genial. He edged his horse close to Boutelle's and extended his hand.

Boutelle tried not to wince at the power of the agent's grip. He managed to return Finley's smile.

Then Finley sighed again.

"Now all we have to do is locate Braided Feather," he said. "Try to find out what the hell is going on."

The dogs were at them first, crashing from the underbrush with angry snarls, lips curled back from yellow fangs, eyes glittering with menace.

Boutelle reined in hard as the running pack began snapping at his horse's legs. His mount began to twist and buck, nickering in alarm, trying to avoid the dogs' teeth. From the corners of his eyes, he saw Finley trying to hold in his mare as well, cursing at the dogs.

Then Apaches were surrounding them, pointing rifles, dark faces impassive. The dogs drew back, still snarling, as Finley spoke to the threatening braves.

At first it seemed it wasn't going to work; the Indians

raised their rifles as though to fire.

Then Lean Bear appeared from the woods and, seeing Finley, ordered off his men. Finley thanked him.

"Why are you here?" Lean Bear asked suspiciously.

"I must speak to Braided Feather," Finley answered.

"We are not going back to our camp," Lean Bear told him.

"I understand that," Finley replied. "I, too, am concerned about that man and wish to speak to your father about him."

Lean Bear said something in Apache which, Boutelle thought, was obviously spoken in bitter scorn. Then he gestured to Finley for the mare's reins, and Finley tossed them over his horse's head so Lean Bear could grab them.

He looked at Boutelle. "Give them your reins," he said. "And your weapon," he added, slipping his rifle from its scabbard and giving it to Lean Bear, then handing down his pistol.

Boutelle threw the reins of his horse across its head, and a brave took hold of them. Removing his pistol carefully from its holster, he handed it down, butt first, to the Indian's reaching hand, hoping that he wasn't committing suicide by doing so.

The dogs kept circling, growling and baring their teeth as their horses walked skittishly among the Apaches.

"I gather the dogs don't like us," Boutelle said to break the silence.

"They don't like the way we smell," Finley responded.

Boutelle swallowed, looking around. Through the undergrowth, he could see other braves watching them, some armed with rifles, some with bows and arrows.

"What did . . ." His voice faded, and as Finley looked at him, he nodded toward Lean Bear.

"What?" Finley asked.

"What did he say before? He sounded so . . . *scornful*."

"Try *afraid*," Finley said. "When I told him I was concerned about that man, he said, '*Man*?' "

Boutelle shivered at more than the gathering mountain chill. It was beginning to get dark as well. For some reason, he recalled the ghastly screeching noise he'd heard the night before.

He shook away the memory, irritated with himself for being credulous.

"Well, I think he *is* a man," he said, trying to sound as confident as possible.

"Do you?" was all Finley said.

They were moving now into an open glade, deeply shaded by a thick overhead growth of pines. As they entered it, Boutelle saw, in the center of the glade, stacked preparations for a bonfire. He could use a little fire warmth, he thought.

Finley looked at the fire preparations with a sense of foreboding. He knew what it was. Not a camp fire for heat and cooking. It was too big for that.

They were getting ready to light a ceremonial fire.

Boutelle saw more and more of the Pinal Spring band now. How many members did it have? He tried to recall. In the two hundreds, it seemed. He saw clusters of women and children eyeing him and Finley. Never had he felt so alien to an environment, so out of place. This was their world, and he had no comprehension of it whatsoever.

Now the horses were stopped and he and Finley ordered to the ground. They dismounted, and Boutelle realized abruptly that the older man standing in front of them was Braided Feather. He hadn't recognized the chief because here he was not the sternly dignified figure he had been at the treaty meeting. He looked smaller now, more haggard.

Finley moved to the chief and raised his right hand in a saluting gesture. "I come as your friend," he said in Apache.

"We know you are our friend," Braided Feather answered. "Come with me."

He led them away from the other Apaches to a small shelter that had been erected for him. He sank down on a buffalo robe beneath the overhang and gestured for them to sit. Boutelle glanced around and saw that Lean Bear had followed them. He looked back at the other Apaches and saw that they were tying up the two horses.

"First let me tell you what the Army and the citizens of Picture City think," Finley said to the chief as Lean Bear sat down with them.

"No need," Braided Feather replied. "I know what they think. That we have broken the treaty."

"Yes." Finley nodded.

Boutelle wished that he understood what they were saying but felt awkward about asking Finley to interpret.

"Does Finley think this as well?" Braided Feather asked the agent.

"Of course I don't," Finley answered. "I know you to be a man of your word. I know that this is something else."

"It is." Braided Feather's lips tightened. "Something very different."

"Can you tell me what it is so I can help?" Finley asked.

Braided Feather looked at his son, who looked toward the fire area and the Apaches waiting around it.

"There is no time," Braided Feather said.

"What is the ceremony to be then?" Finley asked, having noticed Lean Bear's look.

Boutelle had no idea what was being said, but when Finley spoke, he was aware that both Braided Feather and Lean Bear grew tense.

"I cannot tell you that," Braided Feather told Finley. "It is big medicine."

"May we watch so we can learn and perhaps assist you in this?" Finley asked.

Lean Bear stiffened visibly and looked at Finley in anger. "This is not possible," he said.

Finley looked at Braided Feather, knowing that despite Lean Bear's position as eventual chief of the Pinal Spring band, all authority was still in the chief's hands.

"I know it is much to ask," he said, "but this is not an ordinary circumstance. I know that something very dark is taking place and want to help if I can. Are you certain you can deal with this alone?"

Boutelle flinched as Lean Bear spoke sharply to his father, then to Finley. Braided Feather was patient with him at first, but as his hotheaded son spoke with more and more vehemence, his father suddenly cut him off and clearly ordered him to move away.

Lean Bear grimaced savagely and lurched to his feet. "This is a bad mistake," he said and strode away quickly.

Finley looked at Braided Feather without speaking. He knew that to say—particularly to ask—any more would be a slight to the chief's position. Accordingly, he waited in respectful silence.

Finally, Braided Feather spoke. There was a sound of sadness in his voice, Boutelle thought.

"You know that my son is right," the chief said. "This is not a ceremony we permit outsiders to witness." Finley felt a chill to hear a waver in Braided Feather's voice. "But this is *not* an ordinary thing, as you have said. It may well be I am forced to ask for your help. This being so . . ."

He stopped and sighed heavily. "We begin when darkness falls," he said.

Boutelle didn't realize that they had been dismissed until

Finley took him by the arm and helped him to his feet.

As they walked away from Braided Feather's shelter, he asked Finley what the conversation had been about.

When Finley told him, Boutelle frowned, not understanding. "All that over a ceremony?"

"White men are never permitted to witness such Apache ceremonies," Finley told him. "They are a very religious people and their ceremonies are sacred to them. The only reason we're being permitted to look at this particular ceremony is that Braided Feather thinks we might help in this situation."

"We?" Boutelle looked dubious.

"All right, me," Finley admitted. He drew in a deep breath. "This is a very special ceremony," he said. "What they call *big medicine*. Extremely important. I still can't believe they're going to let us watch."

"Why did you ask then?" Boutelle asked.

"Frankly, I don't know," Finley told him. "What's happening is so . . . *distant* from anything I've ever seen that I've behaved in a different manner with the chief. A manner I never would have assumed under more normal circumstances."

They walked in silence toward the fire area. Boutelle looked up. The sky, now barely visible through the pine growth overhead, was almost dark.

"Keep in mind," Finley told him, "these are brave men. Brave women. And they're terrified of something. Absolutely terrified. What else would make them flee their camp to perform a nighttime religious ceremony in the high woods?"

Boutelle glanced into the eyes of Apache men, women, and children as he passed them. Was it his imagination that he saw cold dread in every one of them?

# Thirteen

HE HAD NEVER experienced anything so strange in his life.

In the near pitch-blackness of the glade, the deep, resonant voice of the band's shaman seemed to be coming at him from all directions. The fact that the shaman was speaking in the guttural, rhythmic language of the Apaches which he could not understand in any way made it all the more bizarre to Boutelle as he sat there on the pine needle-covered ground.

He and Finley were located far back from the others so that the Indian agent could interpret for him. In the darkness of the forest, even Finley's whispering voice sounded unnaturally loud to Boutelle. He felt immersed in some grotesque dream, while at the same time knowing that he was totally awake.

"He's telling them that they are all in mortal danger," Finley whispered into Boutelle's ear. "He says that he's going to perform a rite of scourging to prevent this danger from destroying them, man, woman, and child."

Boutelle swallowed. His throat was dry and he felt a strong need for a sip of water, yet knew it was impossible right now. Feeling almost numb, he sat immobile listening, as Finley continued.

"He's telling them that they must give this ceremony undivided attention and never smile or laugh or do a single thing to displease him or he'll be forced to call a halt to the rite, leaving them unprotected."

Smile? Boutelle thought. Laugh? Who could possibly do either under these conditions?

"The ceremony will first inform them how this terror came to be," Finley finished.

Boutelle shivered. In the darkness, fear comes far too easily, he thought. No wonder nighttime was the time when terror flourished.

The shaman had stopped speaking now. In the heavy silence, Boutelle heard only faint rustling sounds as the waiting Apaches shifted slightly on the ground, a few of them coughing softly.

"Who was speaking?" he asked Finley in a whisper, more to hear the sound of his own voice than out of curiosity.

"The band's shaman," Finley replied.

"How did he become that?" Boutelle asked.

"By receiving a power grant from the mountain spirits in a vision experience," Finley answered matter-of-factly.

Boutelle was about to respond, then changed his mind. How could one respond to such a statement? It was too far beyond the world he knew and accepted.

He started as a fire brand seemed to burst forth from nowhere. He saw it moving in the darkness like a flaming insect.

Then the bonfire was ignited and its stacked wood flamed up with a crackling roar.

Now he could see the Apaches gathered in a giant circle around the mounting fire, all of them seated cross-legged, their faces reflecting the flames like burnished oak, their dark eyes glowing as they stared at the fire. Who *were* they? he wondered. What were they thinking? Once again, he felt completely foreign to the moment, trapped in some unearthly vision.

He glanced at Finley. The agent was looking steadily toward the fire. Even he seemed alien to Boutelle now. Clearly, Finley was a part of all this, accepting what was happening without question. An odd image flitted across Boutelle's mind: him dancing at a New York City ball, wearing dress clothes, chatting casually.

The image seemed a million miles and years from this experience.

His legs jerked in reflexively as drums began to thud with a slow, regular beat, one-two-three-four, one-two-three-four.

He looked toward the fire. The shaman was standing beside it. Boutelle could see now how very old the man was, his coarse black hair streaked with gray. He was beginning to speak, his voice rising and falling with a sound reminiscent of the cries of coyotes. He wondered what the shaman was saying.

Finley looked intently at the medicine man as he spoke. The old man was beginning the history of a creature named Vandaih.

First a tall brave emerged from the darkness, moving to the beat of the drums. He danced in erratic circles as though deranged or drunk. When other braves appeared, he withdrew from its sheath a long knife and began to slash symbolically at them. The other braves clutched at their chests and fell to the ground in convulsing death.

Vandaih continued dancing, his expression one of maddened glee. Figures dressed as women danced from the darkness to the one-two-three-four beat of the drums, and Vandaih clutched at them, taking them in symbolic rape.

Finally, two braves grabbed him from each side and forced him into the darkness as the shaman spoke of how Vandaih, for all his sins against his people, had to suffer condemnation.

Boutelle leaned over to ask what was happening, and Finley quickly told him.

He was in the middle of a sentence when they both jumped and Finley's voice broke off as a figure leapt clumsily into the firelight.

The figure was that of a giant bird, its wings made from branches, its head a crude mask which emphasized its curving beak, the figure barefoot, toes curled in to approximate the look of talons.

As the shaman spoke, Boutelle leaned in to whisper in Finley's ear, "What's happening?"

"As condemnation for his grievous sins," Finley told him, "the tribe medicine man turned Vandaih into an eagle."

Boutelle felt a momentary sense of derision relaxing him. An *eagle*? he thought. All this about some ancient Indian transformed into an eagle?

It wasn't over though. The history continued as the eagle form danced crazily in the firelight, twisting in apparent agony and thrashing its giant wings.

"Vandaih, desperate in his blighted loneliness," the shaman continued, "conceived a hideous plan."

Another dancer, dressed as a woman, materialized from the darkness, and after moving with her in a grotesque dance of courting, the eagle suddenly grabbed her and dragged her off into the night.

"He carried off a woman who was not an Indian but whose skin was white," Finley whispered to Boutelle, repeating what the shaman had said.

Boutelle shuddered, angry at himself for doing so. This is ridiculous, he thought. Each new element of the history was more preposterous than the one before.

He leaned close to Finley and told him so.

Was that a smile of amusement on the agent's lips? It seemed too ominous for that.

"If you think everything that's happened up to now is ridiculous," Finley whispered, "you're going to love this new part." The smile, Boutelle now saw, was definitely not one of amusement.

The man dressed as a woman reappeared and from beneath her bulky costume drew forth what Boutelle took to be—

"A *child*?" he whispered incredulously. "He's telling us there was a child?"

The woman moved into the darkness, carrying the child form.

"Thus this child whose father was an eagle and whose mother was a white woman grew to manhood," the medicine man continued. Finley decided not to translate his words to Boutelle. The young man was having trouble enough as it was. He only wished he could be equally disdainful. On the face of it, it was absurdly superstitious. Still, all these things had happened in the past two days. Things there was no way of denying, much less explaining.

And here in the darkness of this forest glade, with the crackling fire and the endless four-beat thudding of the drums and the silent forms of the Apaches as they sat and watched and undoubtedly believed, it was virtually impossible to deny it.

He flinched as another figure jumped out from the darkness.

"So grew to manhood the issue of this unholy union," the shaman went on. "Vandaih, the man now cursed to be for all time an eagle, its father; the abducted and ravished white woman, its mother."

The man now spun abruptly into the darkness to return seconds later, holding wings, a grotesque mask across his face.

"This malevolent child was capable in times of anger or fear of changing himself at will, of sprouting great black wings instead of arms, of creating talons where his hands had been and dreadful, beaked features for a face. In short, to be a hideous creature, part man, part eagle."

Finley felt obliged to pass along this information, even knowing what Boutelle's reaction would most likely be. He whispered into the young man's ear and saw from Boutelle's scowl that his reaction was exactly as expected.

"Do you *believe* all this?" Boutelle demanded of him, his voice loud enough to make Finley shake his head in warning. Boutelle withdrew into angry silence, unable to tell whether it was truly anger that shook him or dread. Was his disbelief becoming more intense the closer he came to losing it?

He started again as an Apache, garbed as a shaman, leapt from the darkness followed by six braves who grabbed the half man-half eagle form and held him by his lashing wings while the shaman drew a knife with a black blade from beneath his robe and appeared to plunge it into the eagle man's chest.

"The people, through the intervention of their medicine man," Finley whispered to Boutelle, "managed to kill the halfling son by stabbing him to death with an obsidian blade, the only substance able to pierce his accursed skin."

He didn't look to see what Boutelle's reaction to that was. He already knew.

The eagle man, now limp, was dragged into the darkness. In a matter of seconds, the braves and their shaman returned, moving, as always, to the one-two-three-four beating of the drums. They carried in their arms what looked like torn pieces of bird and man.

"They also killed Vandaih and the halfling's mother to prevent their further union," the shaman said. "The son, part man, part eagle, they beheaded, burying at separate, distant points the halfling's head and body."

Finley interpreted. Boutelle closed his eyes, trying to resist the rise of cold foreboding in himself. But all he could think of—a chilling memory in his mind's eye—was the thick, jagged scar around the stranger's neck, a scar which could well mark a deep cut that—

No! He bit his teeth together so rabidly that streaks of pain shot through his jaw. He would not allow himself to believe—

He opened his eyes and looked at the fire in dismay.

A small man garbed in black was dancing in the firelight to the one-two-three-four pulsing of the drums. He tried to block his mind from sensing who the figure represented as the shaman spoke. Don't tell me, he thought, silently addressing Finley. But the agent, never pausing, leaned over to translate. "An eon of moons later, a little man with white skin and brightly curious eyes—a man of schooling—came to our Pinal Spring band and requested to see feats of magic performed by the tribal shaman."

The shaman himself approached the little man in black and, clutching him by the arm, forcefully ejected him into the night. As he did, he spoke, "I told this man named Dodge that what he asked was not a thing we could provide. The man was thrust away in anger."

Boutelle felt cold now, almost sick. He tried to resist the mounting disquiet, but it was becoming more and more difficult for him. Too many elements were falling into place. The history of some ancient happening was now a history of today, too close to ignore, much less reject.

The drumbeat—one-two-three-four, one-two-three-four—seemed to alter his heartbeat, taking it over as he watched the small man in black circle the fire and finally come upon an old man seated in the shadows. *Don't tell me*, he thought, but knew it was in vain as Finley translated the grimly voiced words of the shaman.

"The small man with the bright eyes would not be dissuaded, traveling to the far-off dwelling place of the Night Doctor."

For the first time since the ceremony had begun, Boutelle heard a shocking intake of breath from the watching members of the band. The shaman threw them an angry glance but clearly felt that their reaction to this information was justified for he did not rebuke them further, but only went on with his story. Boutelle sat in stricken silence, listening to Finley's whisper, knowing that he was unable now to fight away acceptance of this dreadful history.

"The Night Doctor had been banished from the tribe for tampering with evil powers," the shaman continued, even though he knew his people were aware of this, Finley understood.

The small man in black feigned putting coins into the palm of the Night Doctor, who nodded. Boutelle shook as the drumbeat started to increase in speed though still retaining, endlessly, the one-two-three-four rhythm.

"And, for the gain of Dodge's money, the banished Night Doctor performed an abominable rite," the shaman said. Finley translated the words into Boutelle's ear.

His heartbeat had increased now, driven by the mesmerizing beat of the drums. One-two-three-four—faster, faster. Boutelle sat frozen, staring at the scene taking place at the fire.

The Night Doctor summoning back from the dead the son of Vandaih and joining head to body.

He shuddered as the small man in black leapt off into darkness, bolting from the invocation, causing the Night Doctor's dance to become one of horror as the eagle man escaped.

"The small man, terrified by what he saw—the connecting of the halfling's head to its body—fled the ceremony," the shaman said, "destroying, by that flight, the Night Doctor's control of the ritual and permitting the son of Vandaih to break from his control and move freely in the world again."

Boutelle felt the cold fingers of his hands twitching on his lap as he watched the man portraying the Night Doctor sprinkle some kind of dust over himself and whirl into the darkness.

"The Night Doctor could only cast a spell upon himself and gain protection from the halfling."

The eagle man now leapt into the firelight again, dancing in a fury.

"The son of Vandaih, maddened by frustration, was unable to locate the Night Doctor and destroy him so that he could assure his freedom for all time.

"So the halfling set out instead to find the small man, Dodge. The only person who might take him to the hiding place of the Night Doctor."

Finley stopped repeating the shaman's words into Boutelle's ear, and they sat in motionless silence as the scourging rite commenced.

There was an audible stir from the watching members of the band as ritual dancers appeared from the darkness, four masked figures wearing painted wooden headdresses, short buckskin skirts, and moccasins, their bodies naked from the waist up and painted black, white, green, and yellow. They danced around the circle to the one-two-three-four beat—now slow again—as though searching for something.

Boutelle winced as he looked at the dancer's *gaan* masks, the laths of which were made of split yucca secured to each other and to supporting framework pieces with buckskin thongs. The U-shaped headpieces slid down on each side of their heads with only slits for eyes and mouth. The colorful headdresses had snakes painted on them.

Boutelle was back in the dream again as he watched the dancers moving in unison to the constant thudding of the drums. They each held matching wands made of sotol laths with three crosspieces with which they gestured as they danced. Boutelle's eyes slipped out of focus and he saw, in front of him, four shapeless forms moving like figures in his dream, the beat of the drums pervading his brain and body.

He started, focusing his eyes again, as another figure suddenly appeared, dancing around the four. He wore a G-string around his middle, the upper part of his body coated with white clay. Like the other dancers, he wore a mask with slits for eyes and mouth. The headdress of his mask was larger, though, with long wing feathers of an eagle as the upright pieces. In his hand he carried the middle tail feathers of an eagle, and the other dancers averted their faces from him.

"Who is he supposed to be?" Boutelle leaned over to whisper.

"The Black One," Finley told him. "A special kind of mountain spirit who protects the Apaches and their territories."

Boutelle nodded, staring at the dancers. Once again, the drumbeats seemed to have taken control of his heart so that he felt a part of the ceremony, as though his consciousness was being absorbed by the sight and sound of it.

He felt himself tensing as the dancers started throwing powder in the air and in the fire where it sparked like short-lived fireflies. He wanted to ask Finley what they were doing but didn't have the strength.

Finley seemed to read his thoughts and leaned in close to whisper, "That's cattail pollen they're throwing. Very important as a ceremonial offering to Usen to help them resist the powers of the halfling."

Usen? Boutelle thought. Again, Finley seemed to read his mind. "The giver of life," he whispered.

Boutelle thought he nodded but didn't. He sat unmoving, barely conscious of his body, attention fixed on the ritual dancers as they circled the dwindling fire, the Black One sometimes leading, other times following. Boutelle noticed that whenever the Black One passed in front of the observing Apaches, they lowered their heads as though afraid to look at him.

He kept sinking deeper and deeper into a thoughtless state, almost stupefied, his eyes held fast to the movement of the fire-lit dancers as they danced in unison to the hypnotic one-two-three-four rhythm of the drums.

He barely stirred as the shaman now appeared, clearly addressing the Black One. He had no idea what the shaman was saying, although he assumed that it was some form of request for protection by the Black One.

Only Finley understood the words as the medicine man first praised the Black One for his strength and omnipotence, then told him what he had to do to the evil and curse-laden son of Vandaih: Tear him into a hundred pieces and bury them at the four corners of the earth, sinking the halfling's head in the deepest waters of the deepest sea.

Boutelle's legs twitched, his glazed eyes blinking suddenly as Finley took him by the arms.

"Come," the agent murmured.

Boutelle almost fell as he stood, his legs without feeling. Then, as Finley supported him, he started walking stiffly with the agent around the outside edges of the still-continuing ceremony.

"What is it?" he asked.

Finley didn't answer, only guided the younger man across the border of the forest floor.

"What is it?" he repeated.

Finley pointed ahead with his free hand. Looking in that direction, Boutelle saw, by the peripheral light of the fire, the figure of Braided Feather moving toward his shelter.

"Why is he leaving the ceremony?" he asked.

"Why indeed?" Finley questioned back.

The old chief looked around as they approached, his expression grave. Boutelle listened as Finley spoke with the chief. Then Finley turned away, leading Boutelle from the shelter.

After they'd walked some yards, Finley sat down and leaned against a pine trunk. Boutelle sat beside him, wondering what was happening. In the distance, he could see the ritual still taking place, the firelight now waning noticeably.

"Finley, what is it?" he asked.

The agent sighed. "It's all a waste of time," he said.

"What?"

"The ceremony."

"I don't understand," Boutelle responded. "Then why are they—"

"To keep their people from total panic," Finley said. "But the shaman and Braided Feather know that the ritual is pointless."

Boutelle stared at him, not knowing what to say.

"The Night Doctor brought this on," Finley told him. "He invoked the demon and only he can put an end to it."

# Fourteen

DESPITE HIS EXHAUSTION, Boutelle had been unable to fall asleep for more than an hour and a half. He had lain awake on the buffalo robe Braided Feather had let them use, beneath the heavy wool blanket Finley was sharing with him. He was warm enough and tired enough to sleep under any circumstance.

Except the one he was living through.

He was amazed—impressed even—that Finley had gone to sleep in what seemed to him to be only a few seconds. He decided that men "out here" were able to do that, blank their minds to imminent peril and find much needed sleep in order to face that peril, rested.

He was not cut from that bolt of cloth. His mind, aroused by dread and apprehension, refused to release him. It kept running like an overwound clock, ticking out endless minutes of thoughts and anxieties.

He kept reliving the ceremony performed by the Apaches. It seemed bizarre to him that Braided Feather and his medicine man—undoubtedly his son Lean Bear as well—could permit the ritual to take place, knowing all the time that it was pointless and in vain.

Beyond that, he could think only of the menace they all seemed convinced they were facing—the son of Vandaih. Could he possibly accept such an incredible notion? A man who in moments of fear or anger could become a creature part man, part eagle?

Over and over, logic sought to dispel the farfetched idea.

Even here in the dark forest, deep within Indian country, utterly removed from any aspect of civilization, he found it virtually impossible to believe.

A *demon*?

He tried not to move about in restless distress because Finley lay beside him, heavily asleep. Still, he turned from his left side onto his back, onto his right side, finally onto his back again, eyes staring up at what little sky he could see through the heavy foliage overhead, the thin sprinkling of diamond-white stars.

Invoked a *demon*? he thought.

"For God's sake," he mumbled more than once. He was a graduate of Harvard, for God's sake. This was the nineteenth century, for God's sake. Such things did not take place. Demons belonged in fairy tales, in witches' dungeons, in tales of farfetched horror.

Not in the real world, in real life.

His transition into sleep came unnoticed. He was thinking of the so-called creature, then in the next moment, he was speaking about it to Finley as they sat on the edge of a high cliff looking across a massive forest top that stretched immeasurably into the distance.

"Is it safe for us to sit here like this?" he asked. "Aren't we inviting trouble?"

"Of course," Finley replied. "That's exactly what I want. To lure him into our trap."

"What trap?" he asked. "What can *we* do?"

"I have a little something in mind," Finley said.

"Well, that *sounds* good, but what does it *mean*?" he demanded. "How are we supposed to overcome some creature who can—"

"Hold it." Finley grabbed his arm. "I think I hear it coming."

This is madness! Boutelle thought. No matter what Finley

said, they had no defense against a creature of such deadly power.

"Finley, I think we'd better—"

It was all he had time to say before a giant, shadowy form came swooping down from above and crashed against them both. Suddenly he could feel the feathery softness of wing feathers against his face and what felt like sharp talons gripping his shoulders.

"Finley!" he screamed.

But the horrendous screech of the eagle man drowned out his voice.

Boutelle jerked awake, sitting up with wide eyes, his heartbeat pounding.

The horrendous screech was real. He heard it again and again. And something else, something infinitely more hideous.

The screams of a dying horse.

He looked around groggily as Finley leapt to his feet.

"What is it?" he asked.

Finley didn't answer, lunging away from him, moving in the direction of the screaming animal.

Boutelle scrambled to his knees and pushed up quickly, staggering a little as he stood. It was still dark in the forest, despite a faint pallor of light in the sky.

He started running after Finley. Tripping on a tree root and almost sprawling, he felt a sting of pain where the snake had bitten him. Then it was gone and he was after Finley again, face a twisted mask of dismay as he heard the horrible screams of the horse—which abruptly ended.

Now he saw that the Apaches were awake as well, some of the braves running the same way as Finley, others milling around in frantic alarm, women and children staring, some of them crying. What in the name of God? he thought.

He gasped in alarm as an Apache pony came lunging at him from the darkness. Flinging himself to the right, he barely escaped being hit, so close to the galloping horse that he felt the breeze of its passing. He stumbled, almost fell, then regained his footing. As he continued after Finley, he saw the shadowy forms of other ponies racing through the Apache camp. Clearly, they had been stampeded by terror.

He found Braided Feather and Lean Bear standing with Finley and some braves around the remains of the horse.

His.

He looked in sickened horror at the torn, bloody carcass. It was as though it had been slashed apart by giant razor blades, bleeding flesh exposed, glistening entrails ripped from place. The horse's eyes were wide and staring; there was foam across its jaws.

Finley was looking upward. There was an opening in the trees above where the horses had been tied. The faintly dawning sky was clearly visible. Plenty of room for some flying thing to descend on the horses, Boutelle thought.

He looked back at the butchered animal, twitching with a faint cry as a final death spasm shook its torn, blood-splattered body. What did this? It was all he could allow himself to think, trying not to admit to himself that he knew exactly what had done it.

He looked over at Finley. It made him all the more frightened to see the expression on the agent's face. Sickened. Dazed.

Helpless.

"There is only one solution to this," Finley said to Braided Feather. "Someone has to find the Night Doctor and force him—"

"*Ask* him," Braided Feather interrupted. "He will not be

forced. It is this very thing about him which brought on the horror in the beginning."

"I understand." Finley nodded. "What I mean to say is that we all know the horror will not end until the Night Doctor ends it."

"No man in my tribe will dare to face this," Braided Feather told him.

Finley said, "Then I will."

It was silent in the forest. Even though it was well past dawn, shadowy darkness still prevailed beneath the thick overhanging of the pine trees. Finley and Boutelle were sitting with the chief. The horses had been gathered back, the dead horse carried off for disposal, Lean Bear and his scouts sent out to observe the terrain—and the sky—in all directions. Boutelle wondered what Finley and the chief had been saying but didn't dare ask.

Braided Feather finally spoke.

"You would do this?" he asked, almost in disbelief.

Finley's smile was grim. "I don't want to," he said, "but I *am* the agent for this territory. I am committed to protect the Apaches."

He smiled again, this time adding a rueful sound.

"I never thought my duties would include something like this," he said. "Still . . ." The smile was gone. "I'm willing to try. Someone has to try."

Braided Feather leaned toward Finley, reaching out to grasp his arm. "You are very brave," he said. "I salute your bravery."

"Salute me if it works," Finley told the chief. "Have you any idea at all where the Night Doctor might be?"

"Somewhere in the mountain caves, we believe," Braided Feather told him.

Finley nodded. "Could I take the robe of the buffalo with me then?" he asked. "It is very cold up there."

Braided Feather nodded. "Take it with our blessing," he said.

"Thank you." Finley stood, Boutelle following his lead.

"Wait," Braided Feather said.

The agent and Boutelle stood waiting while the chief looked through his belongings. Finally he unwrapped a wolf-hide covering to reveal a long knife.

Its blade was as dark as night.

He handed it to Finley. "Take this," he said. "It is the only protection I can give you."

"Obsidian?" Finley asked.

The chief nodded.

Finley removed a long knife from its scabbard on his left side. He held it out to Braided Feather. "Hold this, please, until I return with your knife," he said.

Braided Feather nodded. "I will hold it," he said.

As they moved away from Braided Feather's shelter, they saw preparations being made by the Pinal Spring band to leave the camp.

"Where can they go?" Boutelle asked. He added something else which Finley didn't hear.

Finley glanced at the younger man. "What was that last?" he asked.

At first, it seemed as though Boutelle wasn't going to answer. Then he said, very quietly, "If it can fly."

Finley looked at him again. "You *do* believe it then," he said.

"I . . . don't know," Boutelle faltered. "I don't *want* to believe it and yet . . ." He shook himself. "I guess I'll have to ride with you," he said. "My horse—"

"That's impossible," Finley cut him off.

"What?" Boutelle looked at him in surprise.

"I'll be going by myself," Finley said.

"What are you talking about?" Boutelle asked.

Finley told him what he planned to do. The younger man was dumbfounded. "By yourself?" he asked.

"The Apaches are too frightened to go," Finley said. "Someone has to try. It's the only chance."

"That's insane," Boutelle responded, but his voice was so soft and devoid of resolve it undid his words.

They reached their grounded saddles, and Boutelle watched the agent gather together his belongings.

At last he said, "Do you think the chief will let me have one of their horses?"

Finley didn't even look up. "That's impossible, too," he said.

"Why?" Boutelle demanded. "Why is it impossible?"

"Because there's no point in both of us committing suicide," Finley answered.

Boutelle stared at him. "Is that what you think you're doing?" he asked. "Committing suicide? How is that going to help the Apaches?"

Finley sighed. "I was exaggerating to make a point," he said. "I have this." He patted the hilt of the obsidian knife.

"What *is* that?" Boutelle asked. "I wondered when the chief gave it to you."

Finley explained about the knife, Boutelle remembering the ceremony, not reassured by his words. If anything, he looked more aghast. "That's it?" he asked. "Against . . . ?" Clearly, he could think of no way to describe the son of Vandaih.

"No, that isn't it," Finley said. "My plan is to find the Night Doctor and have him . . . *revoke* the creature."

Boutelle simply couldn't take in the insanity of it all. He could deal only with one small aspect of it at a time and that he was certain about.

"I'm going with you," he said.

Finley looked up almost angrily, words set to spill from his lips, words of rejecting, discouraging, absolute refusal.

Then he saw the look on Boutelle's face and a panoramic vision of what would surely take place if he continued arguing swept across his mind. He would refute and argue, refuse and deny, and at every turn, Boutelle would counter him with stubborn insistence. He saw all that in the younger man's obdurate look, the expression of a man who, reaching a point-of-no-return decision, cannot be made to change his mind.

There simply wasn't time for that. At any rate, it was no problem anyway.

"All right, you can go," he told Boutelle. "If we can talk Braided Feather into letting you use one of their ponies."

He knew that would never happen. The Apaches were short of horses, many already doubling to ride.

"That won't be necessary," Boutelle answered.

Finley looked at him, frowning. What was Boutelle talking about now?

Then he saw the younger man gazing off to their left, and he turned and looked.

Lean Bear was riding into camp, leading Professor Dodge's Appaloosa.

The professor's limp body was draped across the horse's back behind the saddle.

Finley and Boutelle moved quickly to where several Apache braves and their chief were converging on the pair of horses. Lean Bear stopped his mount, lifted his right leg over the horse's back, and slid to the ground.

"Where did you find him?" Braided Feather asked his son. Finley couldn't understand how the chief knew who it was. It had been years since Dodge made his refused request. Did Braided Feather still remember Dodge's face from that long ago?

"At the foot of the mountains," Lean Bear answered. Finley noted without surprise that neither he nor his father looked directly at Dodge.

He moved to Dodge's body and lifted his head. Boutelle, beside him, hissed with shock.

"That look again," Finley said.

Boutelle swallowed. For several moments, he was sorely tempted to reverse his stance about going with Finley. The agent wouldn't say a thing if he rode back to Picture City on Dodge's horse. It would probably relieve him.

He forced away the impulse. No, he thought.

"I'll be riding the professor's horse," he said to Finley.

The agent didn't respond. He didn't have the strength to argue with Boutelle now. Actually, he was grateful that he wouldn't be alone. He began to untie the professor's body from its place on the horse's back, thinking darkly that in all likelihood he would never see Picture City again.

# SATURDAY

# Fifteen

IT WAS ALREADY nearing sunset. Boutelle could not believe how fast the day had gone by. They had never even stopped to eat, chewing on jerky and sipping from canteens as they rode.

He tried not to look to his left. The drop from the narrow ledge was prodigious. He was impressed—as well as overwrought—by the way his horse picked its way along, the hooves of its front and rear left legs scant inches from the brink of the winding ledge. Occasionally, it slipped, making Boutelle freeze with apprehension. Then it caught itself, regaining balance and moving on calmly. He envied its ability to instantly forget near death. Or did it need to forget? Perhaps it was essentially unaware of its ongoing peril. Wish I could say the same, he thought.

He'd stopped looking over his shoulder to see if Finley was still behind. He was afraid that if he did, he'd lose equilibrium and slip. His gaze shifted to Lean Bear riding ahead of him.

They—especially Finley—had been startled when the chief's son had chosen to lead them into the mountains. Obviously he was as terrified of the son of Vandaih as all the others in his band.

When Finley had asked him why he was doing it, Lean Bear had answered (Finley later told Boutelle) that they would never find the Night Doctor without his help.

Knowing his dread, Finley had thanked him, commending him for his courage.

"I am not doing this for you that you need thank me," Lean Bear had responded coldly. "I do it for my people."

"I understand and appreciate," Finley had said without rancor.

Lean Bear had relented slightly then. "You are an honest man, Finley," he'd said. "A brave one."

He'd added then with renewed coldness in his voice, "It is men like *him*"—he'd glanced at Boutelle—"who have brought doom to my people."

Finley hadn't told Boutelle that part when the man had asked what Lean Bear had gone on to say. Finley had told him that the chief's son had said (which he had) that it was bad enough what the white man had done to his people, now a white man (Dodge) had brought down upon their heads the wrath of this demon creature.

Remembering that, Boutelle shivered and pulled the buffalo robe closer around himself. Thank God Braided Feather had given robes to him and Finley. It was getting colder by the moment, the canyon walls scourged by an endless, icy wind that seemed to slash at his face like tiny, frozen razor blades.

He gazed up briefly at the canyon wall. It looked as though it had been hacked into shape by giant, frenzy-driven pick blows. A reddish cast was inching across it, causing shadows to shift and disappear, then reappear in other places.

Was it possible that they would still be on this ledge after darkness had fallen? He could not conceive of anything so terrible. Surely, Lean Bear would find some place for them to stop.

He winced as he saw Lean Bear turn his head to the left and right and slowly scan the sky.

He'd been doing the same thing all day.

Finally, in the middle of the afternoon, Boutelle had

twisted around to speak to Finley.

"If he's so concerned about . . . that *creature*"—he'd been compelled to call it—"following us, why is he wearing a *white* buffalo robe?"

"Because that creature, as you call him, *has* to follow us. He must be close by when the revocation is performed."

"And if he decides to kill us *before* that?" Boutelle had demanded.

"He won't," Finley had said. "He wants us to find the Night Doctor for him so he can kill him before the ceremony. That way he'll be free forever."

Boutelle was chilled by the memory of Finley's words. He'd tried to regain some sense of proportion, recalling his family and his life back East, the total reasonableness of his past.

It didn't work. He was in too deep. He knew that despite all efforts he had come to accept the existence of the son of Vandaih—and the madness of their ride into the mountains to seek out a shaman driven from his people for "tampering."

Boutelle shuddered and looked to his left, unable to prevent himself from doing so.

Gigantic rock formations were now visible in the distance, eroded through eons into separate forms that looked to him like massive statuary, strange figures he could almost make out with imagination, strange faces carved by time and wind and water.

Night was beginning to cover the bases of the huge formations, an ocean of black shadows slowly moving upward on them like a rising lap of dark waters.

Soon the reddish light on the cliffs would diminish, the stone would go gray in the last of twilight, and night would cover them. Then what? Boutelle wondered. Would Lean Bear find a place where they could stop?

And light a fire?

Boutelle shook his head abruptly. No fire, he thought. That would be too easy to spot. They'd be as helpless as that horse had been.

In spite of how it disturbed him, he tilted back his head and looked at the sky.

Had the son of Vandaih been tracking them all day, up so high they couldn't see him, floating on the wind, great wings stretched and motionless, riding the icy currents like a cork on bobbing water, black eyes ever on his prey?

Boutelle glanced over his shoulder, starting slightly as he saw the pale white, shadow-marked circle of the moon. How could it have appeared so quickly? He shivered.

Darkness was almost upon them.

He twitched as Lean Bear abruptly turned and spoke to them.

"The cavern opening is just ahead," Finley told him. "When you see Lean Bear turning into it, follow him fast. We have to hope he doesn't see us disappear."

Boutelle knew exactly who the agent meant by "he" and braced himself to move as he'd been told.

There was no sound but the whistling of the cold wind and the clatter of the horses' hooves on the stone ledge. Moments passed. Lean Bear kept riding forward.

"All right then," Boutelle muttered to himself. Where was the cavern entrance? Why didn't—

The thought broke off, his face tensing in a grimace as Lean Bear suddenly jerked his mount to the right and as though by magic disappeared into the cliff wall.

"Now!" Finley shouted.

Before fear could repress the action, Boutelle drove his knees into the horse's flanks, and, startled, it lurched forward into a trot. Boutelle closed his eyes, convinced that it would slip off the edge, carry him hurtling down into the green valley far below, crushing him on the rocks and . . .

"No," he growled, forcing himself to reopen his eyes.

He had almost missed the cavern entrance. He was forced to jerk the horse around so much that it rose up slightly off its front feet for a horrifying moment. Boutelle was certain that he'd made it lose balance, that it was about to topple backward off the edge.

But at the last moment the horse regained balance and lunged through the opening in the cliff wall. Boutelle hissed as hanging vines whipped across his shoulders and cheeks when he instinctively hunched over and lowered his face.

Inside he pulled in hard on the reins.

The immediate cessation of wind created an illusion of deep silence. Then he heard the sound of hooves—his and Lean Bear's mounts—shifting nervously on the stone floor of the cavern.

He caught his breath, struggling to control his horse as Finley's mount came charging in from outside, bumping against his horse's side, the two animals nickering with alarm.

He and Finley regained control of their mounts, and Boutelle looked around.

There was enough illumination from the sunset—some light seemed to filter in through cracks in the wall—for him to see that the cavern was immense. He had been inside an icehouse in Vermont once, and the air in here was equally as frigid. Even out of the icy wind, Boutelle felt the need to pull the buffalo robe around himself again.

Lean Bear said something, and Finley interpreted.

"He says the Night Doctor will be somewhere in this cavern."

Boutelle only nodded. What was there to say?

"I'd like you to stay here while Lean Bear and I go on," Finley told him.

Boutelle frowned. "Come all this way with you just to stop now?" he replied.

"It could be . . . terrible," Finley said.

Boutelle was about to respond when he realized that his throat had become clogged by fear.

"I'm—" he began. His voice was strangled, and he broke off, wincing. Well, to hell with it, he thought. He cleared his throat with a viscid sound. "I'm not stopping now," he said. His voice was still not normal, but he didn't care. The statement was made.

"David—"

"I am going with you," Boutelle said, determination clearing the sound of his voice.

"We cannot sit and talk," Lean Bear said tensely.

"All right." Finley nodded, sighing. "There isn't time to argue."

"There hasn't been since we left," Boutelle replied.

Finley nodded again and pulled his mount around. "We're ready," he said in Apache.

Lean Bear nodded and reined his pony around, starting into the cavern. Finley followed, Boutelle trailing behind, wondering distractedly what he'd do if he lost track of Finley. You'll die, that's what you'll do, his mind supplied.

Finley was wishing now that he'd talked Boutelle out of coming, forced him to remain behind if necessary. The younger man's goodwill and good intentions would be of little value when—and if—they found the Night Doctor.

For that matter, he wondered what good *his* presence would do when that time came. Since Lean Bear had insisted on leading them, he could also ask the Night Doctor to perform the revocation rite. The Night Doctor had been a part of the Pinal Spring band; Lean Bear was familiar to him. Finley, on the other hand, was a total stranger.

The more he thought about it, the more pointless his presence became in his mind. Which made Boutelle's presence totally senseless. He scowled, then told himself to let it go. What was done was done. He'd made his promise to Braided Feather. That would have to suffice.

He remembered the chief doing something totally unexpected before he'd left. He had embraced Finley, and the feel of the chief's arms and body had made him realize how old and frail Braided Feather really was.

"The future of my people lies with you," the chief had murmured.

Finley had been embarrassed by the chief's show of emotion. Braided Feather had always represented, to him, the epitome of dignity and strength. It had to be the measure of the chief's dread regarding the son of Vandaih that he would display such vulnerable behavior. It had made Finley all the more apprehensive about what he was planning to attempt.

They had gone about a hundred yards through the vast cavern when the light faded into near darkness and Lean Bear stopped to light a torch. The fact that the chief's son had brought the torch along told Finley that he must know the Night Doctor was in here somewhere, or assumed at least that the possibility that he was, was good.

The continuing ride through the cavern was an eerie one.

By the random flicker of the torch in Lean Bear's right hand, Finley could see the walls of the cavern, some dripping with water, some dry. High above, stalactites glimmered, pointing down at them like giant blades. Swords of Damocles, he thought. An appropriate fancy under the circumstances.

He looked back to see if Boutelle was all right. The younger man's expression in the wavering torchlight was a grave one. What was he thinking? Finley wondered. Had he finally come to terms with what was taking place? Or was part of his mind still trying to resist the obvious?

As moments passed, Finley felt himself sinking gradually into a half-conscious reverie, the rhythmic clopping of the horses' hooves on the stone floor of the cavern acting on his mind hypnotically. The flame of the torch ahead became the focal point of his vision as it bobbed along with the movement of Lean Bear's pony. After a while, it was all he could see, and he felt himself begin to weave in the saddle, his progression through the chilly darkness slipping from awareness.

When Lean Bear stopped his mount, Finley almost ran his horse into him; only at the last moment did he blink his eyes, refocusing, and yank back on the reins. He saw Lean Bear looking back at him with disapproving curiosity.

Then the chief's son spoke, the sound of his voice making Finley start a little, it sounded so loud to him.

"He is up ahead," Lean Bear told him.

Finley swallowed dryly, nodding. "All right," he said. "Shall we continue on foot?"

The Apache nodded. "Yes."

As Finley dismounted, he glanced back and saw Boutelle getting off his horse.

"I want you to stay here," he said. He cut off the younger man before he could object. "Lean Bear and I must speak to the shaman. You'd only be in the way."

Boutelle still looked as though he were about to contest Finley's words. But then he nodded curtly. "Very well," he agreed.

Finley grounded his reins and walked to Lean Bear. The chief's son pointed ahead, and Finley, looking in that direction, saw faint light quivering in a corner of the cavern where the overhead roof declined sharply.

It was the light of a fire.

"I will go first," Lean Bear told him. "Walk behind me at a proper distance."

"Very well." Finley nodded.

The two men advanced on the flickering light. When they were ten yards distant from its source, Lean Bear called out, his voice ringing and echoing off the cavern walls, making Finley twitch.

"We are here in peace to see the Night Doctor," the Apache said.

Silence. Lean Bear waited for a short amount of time, then repeated his words.

There was no response.

Is he here? Finley wondered. My God, he thought suddenly, what if the Night Doctor had died of some affliction? He was an old man, older than Braided Feather. He might have had a heart attack, died in his sleep. What would they do if they found only his body?

What *could* they do? he answered himself. It would mean the final release of the creature into the world.

Did the son of Vandaih have to *know* the old man was dead before he could be free?

He tensed as Lean Bear started forward again. Finley drew in a laboring breath and followed him. He looked over his shoulder to make sure Boutelle had remained behind.

The younger man was unseen in the darkness. Finley felt a twinge of concern for him. It had to be unnerving to be left alone in total blackness, in a cavern he could never get out of by himself.

Turning back, he continued after Lean Bear, twitching again as the chief's son spoke loudly.

"We come in peace to see the Night Doctor," he repeated.

Finley almost added, "We will give you pollen and gold for a boon," then decided against it. Lean Bear would be angered by his interference, and he was only guessing that the Night Doctor was acquisitive because he'd taken money from Professor Dodge. That was some time ago. Things had to be different.

They were almost to the fire now. Lean Bear stopped, and Finley moved to his side.

The shaman's living space was scant and primitive. All that was visible was a pair of buffalo robes on the stone floor and an iron pot beside the low fire.

Finley's gaze shifted. Hanging across what clearly was a rift in the outer cave wall was another buffalo robe. But where was the old man? he wondered.

His answer came with the cocking of a rifle hammer to their right. He and Lean Bear looked there quickly.

Standing in a shadowy patch, the Night Doctor had leveled a rifle at them. In the faint glow of the fire reflected on the old man's face, Finley saw the scar-like seams of ninety years marking his skin, his small, dark eyes glittering as he watched them.

"Who *are* you?" he asked, his voice low-pitched and hoarse.

"You know me," Lean Bear told the old man. "I am Lean Bear of the Pinal Spring band. My father—"

"There is no Pinal Spring band," the old man interrupted. "They do not exist."

Finley grimaced. Of course the old man would say that, he thought. He had been driven from the Pinal Spring band. In his mind, they could not possibly exist any longer.

"You know my father, Braided Feather—" Lean Bear started angrily.

"There is no Braided Feather; he does not exist," the Night Doctor cut him off.

Seeing Lean Bear tense and knowing that the old man would not hesitate to shoot him, Finley quickly said, "We have gold and pollen for a boon."

He saw that his words had angered Lean Bear, as he'd expected, but he had to ignore the Apache's reaction. Better he was angry than dead, he thought.

"Who are *you*?" the old man demanded.

"Billjohn Finley," he answered. "Government Indian agent in Picture City."

The Night Doctor gazed at him impassively.

"What boon?" he finally asked.

Lean Bear cut off Finley's voice as he tried to answer the shaman's question.

"You must destroy the son of Vandaih," Lean Bear said.

The old man's reaction was short-lived, albeit unmistakable—momentary shock dispelled by will.

The impassive look returned.

"I do not know any son of Vandaih," he said.

Lean Bear stiffened, leaning toward the old man, only pulling back as the old man raised the rifle to his shoulder.

"You invoked this demon!" Lean Bear lashed out at the shaman. "You must rid the world of him!"

The old man's features twisted suddenly into a mask of savage venom.

"Let the creature live forever!" he cried. "Your people drove me from my wickiup and forced me to this solitary life! I owe you nothing! I delight in your certain destruction, every man, woman and child!"

# Sixteen

THE SHAMAN RAISED the rifle to his shoulder once again.

"Leave," he said. "Or die."

Finley saw, in an instant, that Lean Bear had moved his right hand to the hilt of his knife. The Apache did not intend that the Night Doctor should continue living, even if it cost him his own life.

"If you fire your rifle, the son of Vandaih will hear it," Finley said quickly.

The old man's narrowed eyes shifted to him.

"What do you mean?" he asked.

"Did you think he wouldn't follow us?" Finley said.

The shaman's face grew visibly taut. "You *led* him here?" he asked incredulously.

"How could we do otherwise?" Finley asked. "You know he must be close by when the revocation ceremony is performed."

Hatred twisted the old man's face. "I'll kill you both," he snarled.

"No matter who you kill, the creature knows we're in here," Finley responded. "And you know what he'll do when he finds us—or you."

The shaman drew in a sudden hissing breath through clenched teeth.

"I do not believe you," he said, but there was little confidence in his voice.

"Believe him," Lean Bear said. "I wore the robe of a white buffalo as we rode into the mountains. I watched the sky as we came. High above, so high that I could barely see him, the son of Vandaih followed. The white man speaks the truth. We knew that the creature had to be nearby during the ceremony."

His pitiless smile made coldness move up Finley's spine.

"He is nearby," Lean Bear finished. Then, without a pause, he turned away from the shaman. "We will go now. You have some minutes left to live, perhaps an hour. Then the son of Vandaih will have found you." Another remorseless smile. "I leave it to the eye of your mind what he will do to you."

Finley remained motionless as Lean Bear walked past him. His gaze stayed fixed on the old man's face. The shaman had to be in a state of horror, he thought. Unless he really didn't believe what they said. But how could he not believe when it was obvious that—

"Wait." The Night Doctor's voice told Finley everything, thickened by dread, quavering as an old man's voice would quaver.

Lean Bear turned to face the shaman. He did not speak. Neither did Finley. No need for our words now, he was thinking.

The old man shuddered, lowering the rifle.

"I will perform the ceremony," he said.

Finley, Boutelle, and Lean Bear sat cross-legged on the cave floor, watching silently.

At first, the Night Doctor had informed them that no white man could observe the ceremony he was to perform. Lean Bear had not been opposed to that, but Finley had remained adamant. He and Boutelle had already watched the ceremony performed in the Apache camp, he told the shaman. They were part of this entire situation. They *would* observe.

He knew that under any other circumstances the Night Doctor would refuse to yield. But the old man knew that his time was short, that at any moment the son of Vandaih might burst in on them. He could not take time to argue, so he submitted to Finley's demand. While the shaman gathered what he needed for the ceremony, Finley went and got Boutelle, telling him what had happened.

Now the three men sat in motionless silence, watching the Night Doctor bathe.

The sight of it made Finley restive. If the creature had seen them enter the cavern, he could be close by. The time taken for the old man to wash his body could be fatal to them.

Ironic, too, he thought, a humorless smile drawing back his lips. From the smell of the old man and his living space, cleanliness was not an item high on his list of priorities.

Boutelle leaned over to whisper in his ear, "Why is he doing this?"

"He has to purify himself to ask for help from the Great Spirit," Finley whispered back.

He glanced at Lean Bear. The chief's son was scowling at them. Clearly despite their attempt to be quiet, their words had not eluded the Apache's keen hearing.

His gaze moved back to the Night Doctor.

The old man had finished drying himself and was putting on a short, clean buckskin shirt.

Picking up a small pottery jug (he'd gotten all the ceremony elements from a hidden crevice in the cave) he braced himself visibly, then drank, swallowing deeply. He bent over to put down the jug.

Before he'd straightened up, his face was distorted by a spasm of nausea, and making dreadful, gagging sounds, he lurched to the hanging buffalo robe and swept it aside with a brush of his right arm. He lunged outside just in time to void the contents of his stomach.

"What's he doing?" Boutelle asked, sickened.

"He has to purge himself of all impurities," Finley answered. "There must be no food or drink inside him."

"It doesn't sound likely," Boutelle muttered, grimacing as he listened to the violent retching of the old man outside.

Finley noticed Lean Bear shifting restlessly and knew what he was thinking. It was not completely dark yet and as long as the shaman was outside, he could be seen and there was just the chance—

"For Christ's sake, get back in," he muttered.

He relaxed a little—noticing that Lean Bear did the same—as the Night Doctor came back in, wiping at his lips. The buffalo robe fell back heavily across the opening.

They watched as the old man put on a buffalo robe that had been beaten thin with rocks. The ritual robe, Finley thought.

The shaman worked a leather thong across his head. Hanging from it was a round, metallic medallion with figures inscribed on it. Finley saw from the edge of his vision that Boutelle was looking at him for an explanation. He turned his head and shook it slightly. He dared not speak now. The ceremony was too close.

The Night Doctor had picked up a leather bag and hung it at his waist, its strap diagonally across his bare chest. Then he picked up four pottery dishes with handmade candles in them and placed them at four equidistant points of an invisible circle. These were, Finley knew, the four points of the compass—east, west, north, and south.

Removing a tiny piece of kindling from the fire, the shaman lit the candles.

Then he picked up a deep, dishlike pottery container and scooped up wood coals, dropping them into the container.

Immediately, a thick, greasy smoke began to rise from the dish. Before he had set it down in the center of the circle, the smoke was already starting to fill the cave. Some of it rose toward an opening in the cave roof; some appeared to drift through the hide-covered opening. Finley and Lean Bear both tightened as they saw that. Smoke would be visible for miles.

And it was not yet dark outside. . . .

He bent toward Lean Bear, murmuring, "Must there be such a fire?"

"It is part of the ceremony," Lean Bear responded, but clearly he was nervous about the smoke as well.

"What is it?" Boutelle whispered.

Finley gestured toward the fire, and Boutelle seemed to understand.

"Why doesn't he start?" he whispered, then winced as Lean Bear glared at him.

By then, the Night Doctor was removing articles from another leather pouch and holding them one by one in the smoke from the fire. Boutelle assumed that it was to purify the objects: a wand, a knife, dried plants, a small leather bag, feathers from a large bird. Probably an eagle, Boutelle thought.

Finley looked toward the opening in the wall again. The smoke had thinned, but some was still escaping outside. Get started, he thought urgently. If the son of Vandaih saw that smoke . . .

A shudder ran up his back. They'd be helpless.

He drew in a quick breath and looked at the shaman again, eyes smarting from the greasy pall of smoke in the cave.

The old man was holding something above the smoking fire. It looked to Finley like strips of skin or dried flesh. He had no idea what they were.

Only Lean Bear didn't start as the Night Doctor began to dance around the fire slowly and rhythmically, chanting in his frail, hoarse voice. He had the wand in his left hand, the knife in his right, gesturing with them as he danced first toward the east, then the west, the north, and the south, chanting in each direction.

"O, Usen, O, Great Spirit, you are the sun first rising in the east.

"O, Usen, O, Great Spirit, you are the sun descending in the west.

"O, Usen, O, Great Spirit, you are the winter sun in the north.

"O, Usen, O, Great Spirit, you are the rising sun of spring in the south.

"Spirits of fear and death give way to the sun! This is a place of sanctuary! The roof above, a roof of safety! The floor beneath, a floor of protection!

"O, Usen, O, Great Spirit, protect me from evil approaching from the east, the west, the north, the south."

Finley glanced at Lean Bear, seeing a look of wrath on the Apache's face. He could understand now why the Night Doctor had failed as the shaman of the Pinal Spring band, why they had expelled him.

Ignoring all else, the old man was performing a rite exclusively for his own protection.

And they could do nothing about it.

He had no doubt that the shaman was well aware of their helplessness.

You miserable old bastard, he thought.

He started slightly with Boutelle as the Night Doctor took some powder from the small leather bag and flung it onto the fire. It flashed momentarily, then exuded pale smoke which filled the air with a pungent smell that was sweet and sour at the same time.

Boutelle shook himself, blinking hard and swallowing. The smoke from the burning powder seemed to fill his eyes and throat. He could see the Night Doctor only indistinctly. The old man looked to him like some figure from a mad dream. It seemed as though he could hear the thumping of the drum again. The same one-two-three-four rhythm he had heard in the Apache camp. That was impossible, though. There was no drum. It had to be imagination fixing on the rhythmic thud of the Night Doctor's feet on the floor of the cavern—one-two-three-four, one-two-three-four.

He felt himself beginning to sink again into the trancelike state he'd experienced in the mountain clearing. The sound of the Night Doctor's voice rose and fell in volume and in pitch, sometimes mournful and suppressed, other times aggressive, vehement.

Finley sat rigidly, watching the old man perform his rite of self-protection. He noticed sweat running down the old man's body and became aware of the perspiration on his own face, too, and the many drops of it trickling down his chest and back beneath his shirt.

He winced as the shaman suddenly jabbed at his left palm with the knife blade, drawing blood. Dancing on, he held the palm above the fire, letting dark drops of his blood fall into the glowing wood coals where they hissed.

"O, Usen, O, Great Spirit, let this gift of my blood satisfy and please you that you will protect me from whatever evil is around me."

Soon, the old man would mention the son of Vandaih by name. After the sacrifice. But what would the sacrifice be? Finley tensed, his right hand rising to the hilt of the obsidian knife. The Night Doctor was sapped by age. Still . . .

His hand lowered again as the shaman danced to a nearby corner of the cave and pulled a wolf's hide from a bulky object to reveal a cage woven of twigs inside of which a scrawny hen was standing.

The old man's hands moved swiftly. Opening the cage, he seized the chicken by its throat (so it would make no noise, Finley knew) and carried it to the fire, dancing slowly around the smoking dish, extending the struggling hen to the east, the west, the north, and the south.

Boutelle gasped as the shaman, with a blurring movement of his hands, lopped off the hen's head with his knife, then tore the bird in half and dropped its bloody pieces on the fire.

"O, Usen, O, Great Spirit, may the sacrificing of this hen also be accepted by you. May you return this gift by helping me in this time of peril."

What about *us*? Finley thought. Was Lean Bear thinking that as well?

But then the Night Doctor held a folded piece of the animal skin above the fire and chanted, "I have placed the name of Vandaih's son upon this skin, and when I drop this named skin in the fire, you, O, Usen, must, as fire consumes the skin, consume the son of Vandaih, making his body headless and his head bodiless."

Abruptly, he opened the leather bag at his waist and removed something, which he held above the fire. Boutelle felt his stomach twist with nausea.

It was a shrunken, mummified head, and the shaman was swinging it above the fire by its lank, black hair.

"O, Usen, O, Great Spirit, let it be, in this ceremony, that this head is that of the son of Vandaih. O, Usen, please remove this head once more."

Finley felt himself becoming increasingly rigid with anxiety. He'd been wrong. The shaman *did* intend to destroy the son of Vandaih—and the ceremony was approaching its climax. He felt himself leaning forward tensely, eyes fixed on the old man as he danced and chanted in the dim, smoky light, his frail voice more and more agitated.

"O, Usen, who created the night and the day! O, Usen, who created the earth and the skies! O, Usen, who created the darkness and the light! I plead with you to come now and destroy this vile abomination!

"O, Usen, drive away this evil one like dust before the wind! You have the power to crush all things beneath your might! Crush this, my enemy, the son of Vandaih!

"O, Usen, come at once and do what I desire! Let your terrible presence shake the air and destroy the evil that I ask you to destroy! The son of Vandaih, O, Usen! The cursed and murderous son of Vandaih!

"Curse this demon, O, Usen! Hurl him to the bottom of the pit into a lake of fire! First, his foul head, then his foul body, down into the fiery waters of the center of the earth!"

The old man stopped in his tracks and threw up his arms.

"Be gone, son of Vandaih! Be cursed by Usen! Cursed by the earth! Cursed by the sun and the moon and the stars! Cursed—"

He broke off with a gagging sound, face wrenched by sudden mindless terror.

A rush of great wings could be heard outside the cave, a hideous screech, the same screech they had heard while Boutelle's horse was being slaughtered.

"Complete the ceremony!" Lean Bear shouted at the shaman.

But the old man had slumped back onto the cave floor, eyes wide, lips spread, spittle running from his open mouth.

It seemed to Boutelle that everything happened at once. Lean Bear and Finley were on their feet, lunging for the shaman, both crying out at once. The rush of wings became deafening, the ghastly shriek of the creature almost to the opening of the cave. Lean Bear reaching the old man first and clutching at his shoulder, shouting again: Finley repeating the same words.

Lean Bear recoiling in shock and Finley groaning loudly as the old man fell back, dead from fear.

Then the robe across the opening was ripped away, and the huge, winged creature stood before them, face unseen in the shadows. Boutelle had the fleeting impression of a curved beak on its face and talons where its feet should be.

Then all was lost in movement, smoke, and noise as Lean Bear whirled and drew his knife and, with a cry that Boutelle knew was one of hopeless fury, hurled himself at the creature. Abruptly, they were one, a thrashing huge-winged, double-bodied figure, Lean Bear driving his knife into the creature's chest, then screaming out in agony as the creature's head darted forward, its curved beak tearing off the Apache's face.

Twisting around, the creature hurled the dying Indian through the cave opening, and Lean Bear disappeared in darkness, pitched into space and falling to his death without another sound.

Boutelle stiffened, seeing Finley leap toward the creature while its back was turned, the obsidian knife extended in his hand. The agent drove it as hard as he could into the creature's back. But the wings were too thick with heavy feathers and it glanced off a bony rib, barely breaking the creature's skin.

With a cry of pain at the stab of the obsidian blade, the creature twisted back, its left wing smashing across

Finley's outstretched arm, knocking the knife from his grip.

Finley tried to lunge for it, but with a movement so rapid Boutelle could not follow it, one of the creature's taloned feet lashed out and clamped around Finley's right ankle, stopping him abruptly.

The creature started dragging Finley back, its maddened yellow eyes glinting in the firelight.

"*Boutelle*!" Finley cried.

Boutelle moved before his mind could summon the command. Mindlessly, without considering what the pain might be, he grabbed up the fire dish and jumping toward the son of Vandaih, hurled the glowing, smoking contents into the creature's face, seeing at the last moment its huge beak opening to tear off Finley's face.

The creature shrieked in pain as red-hot wood coals sprayed across its head, burning its eyes and setting fire to the dark gray plumage on its face. It staggered back and bumped against the cave opening, only the spread of its wings preventing it from falling through.

In backing off, the creature had been forced to lose its grip on Finley's ankle. Diving across the cave, the agent snatched up the obsidian knife, and before the creature could recover, he leapt up and flung himself at it, driving the black blade deep into its chest until he felt it pierce the creature's heart.

The cave rang with the deafening screech of the creature's death.

Boutelle stumbled back and fell against the cave wall as he saw what happened. He and Finley stared in openmouthed astonishment as they watched the giant wings retracting slowly, saw them thin and disappear into the arm flesh closing up. Saw the creature's beak move slowly into the face and vanish with the plumage. Saw the talons withdraw and change back into human feet.

With that, the son of Vandaih was a man again, the man they'd seen in Picture City, lying dead on the floor of the cave, the obsidian knife buried in his stilled heart, dark blood running down his chest.

Finley slumped down clumsily, and he and Boutelle looked at one another. He felt unable to speak. All he could think of was what he had to do.

But that would have to wait. He couldn't move right now.

At last he spoke.

"You saved my life," he said.

"You saved both of ours," Boutelle responded hoarsely. Not to mention the Pinal Spring band and God knew how many others, he thought. He sat down weakly, closing his eyes. My God, he thought. My dear God.

Several minutes later, Finley struggled to his knees and crawled to the Night Doctor's body. Reaching across him, he picked up the dead Apache's knife and turned back to Boutelle.

"Are you up to this?" he said.

"Do I have any choice?" Boutelle asked.

Finley shook his head slowly. "No," he answered, "I need your help."

"All right." Boutelle nodded. "One thing though."

"What's that?"

"I'll deny, to the end of my life, that I ever did this."

"Don't worry," Finley reassured him with a grim smile, "I'll never mention it, believe me."

Boutelle labored to his feet and moved to the spot where the son of Vandaih lay in motionless silence. He sank to his knees beside the agent.

"All right," he muttered. He filled his lungs with a long, deep breath. "I'm ready," he said.

Finley made the first cut.